I0660930

Bliss Perry

Salem Kittredge, and Other Stories

Bliss Perry

Salem Kittredge, and Other Stories

ISBN/EAN: 9783744661133

Printed in Europe, USA, Canada, Australia, Japan

Cover: Foto ©Andreas Hilbeck / pixelio.de

More available books at **www.hansebooks.com**

Salem Kittredge

and Other Stories

TO MY FATHER

CONTENTS

Salem Kittredge

Theologue

SALEM KITTREDGE,
THEOLOGUE

I.

IT always seemed to Salem Kittredge that his heels clicked more noisily than other men's upon the floor of a hotel office, and this uncomfortable impression was renewed as he stepped up to the desk of the Parker House.

" If Mr. Pitman should call for me, will you tell him that I am here? "

" What name? " said the clerk, without looking up.

" Pitman — J. Howard Pitman. Oh, you mean my name? Mr. Kittredge—Salem Kittredge. It's rather sultry, isn't it? "

" Excuse me? "

" I said it was hot. "

The clerk's only reply to this tentative friendliness was to push back his skull-cap, wipe his forehead, and yawn assentingly. The tall young man in black turned awkwardly away,

3

and walked over to one of the big leather chairs by the window. As he seated himself, he pulled out a silver watch, for the tenth time in the last hour, and found that he still had seven or eight minutes to wait. With a nervously directed handkerchief he flapped the dust of Andover and the B. & M. Road from off his shoes, and then he drew a telegram from his pocket. Once more he read, " Meet me at Parker House, ten o'clock, Thursday, without fail," and wondered again who J. Howard Pitman was, and what he could want of a post-graduate student of theology. In absently folding the telegram, his eye wandered to a newspaper lying on the window-sill. There in the advertising columns was the name that had perplexed him. He had seen it a thousand times: *Pitman's Primitive Pellets*, in audacious type, and underneath it the familiar face—bald, hard-eyed, heavy-mustached—and the scrawled signature.

He was still examining the trade-mark when the proprietor of the pellets hurried in, crossed the office straight toward Kittredge, and put out his hand.

" And you're Salem Kittredge," he said. " Look just like your father, don't you? Your father 'n I used to go to school together up in

Burridge ; little red school-house, just above the Forks. There yet, ain't it? Le' me see, how long is it since your father died ? ''

"Six years," replied Salem, who was still standing, holding Mr. Pitman's hand, and conscious that the clerk was looking at him.

" Well, well ! Now I shouldn't have heard of you at all, if it hadn't been for Professor Bibb—sit down, sit down. Nehemiah Bibb says that you're the young man I'm looking for, he thinks.''

Salem smiled intelligently.

" Bibb came from up in Burridge, too. Knew your father well; and the other day I was telling him what I had in mind, and he said he was sure you'd be just the man." Pitman pushed his chair closer and lowered his voice as he went on. " You see, it's about my boy Freddie—the only boy I've got. He's twenty-three years old next month, but he ain't much of a comfort to me, nor to his mother. He ain't a bad boy—not really a bad boy ; but he has a little—difficulty—Freddie has, and about six or eight times a year he has it rough, I tell you ! He's a nice, pleasant-spoken fellow, and he's keen ; he can run the Works—the Pellet Works, you've heard of 'em ?—as well as I can, when he's straight, and he was always a good

5

scholar when he'd a mind to be. Freddie's all right, when he *is* all right."

"Did he go through college?" inquired Salem, sympathetically. "You spoke of his being a good student."

"One year—almost a year, anyway—and then he had to leave. They didn't want him at Cambridge, they said; they were very polite about it, but they didn't want him."

"It was his scholarship?" ventured Kittredge.

"No, it was a cock - fight;" and a smile quavered a moment under the great mustache. "That was over in Somerville, and that boy— he wa'n't but nineteen—took seven hundred dollars out of Boston men that ought to have known better, and I tell you it went against the grain—just a little against the grain—for me to make him send it back. I don't suppose the fight was any worse—between you 'n me— than one we had once up in Burridge, in your grandfather's barn, when your father and Nehemiah Bibb had their jackknives up on it; but that's neither here nor there.

"So I had to take him out, and he wanted to go on the road," continued Mr. Pitman, "and he doubled our Southern trade in six months. That boy got it into his head that the

6

Pellets would cure fever 'n ague ''—here J. Howard Pitman hesitated, with a whimsical droop of the eyelid and a triumphant twist of his iron-gray mustache—'' and they do cure fever and ague ! There's no doubt about it. They're a specific, and that boy found it out. He has more 'n thirteen hundred signed testimonials from sufferers, up at the Works to-day. He's a hustler, I tell you, when he wants to hustle, but——'' The enthusiasm dropped out of his voice, and his eyes fell to the floor.

Salem was silent, wondering what all this had to do with himself.

'' But just about once in so often,'' the patent medicine man went on slowly, '' about once in two months, Freddie has to take three or four days off, and lets the Pellets roll to Ballyhack, till he gets ready to go on again. I had to go down to Tampa last winter to bring him home, and he came pretty near slipping me in New York as it was. If he'd keep straight and settle down, I'd give him half the business in a minute ; but he don't want to settle yet, he says, and he'll keep on the road, or nothing. I can't get along without him—or with him, and there we are. His mother, she talks to him, but she don't seem to understand Freddie very well—she never did; and our minister's talked to him, and he's just as polite as a boy can be, and just as straight as a boy can be, till the time comes round again, and then everything goes ker-flummux. And here's where you come in. I've had a talk with the doctor about Freddie; the doctor saw him after that Tampa business last winter, and again in May, and he says there's just about one chance for him. ' Your boy,' says he, ' is a confirmed inebriate, or straight on the road to it. It isn't that he wants to drink all the time; he doesn't; he's got the convulsive form of acute alcoholism. You must get a good, steady young fellow to go to Europe with him, or round the world, or somewhere, and watch him night and day when these turns are coming on. If he gets by one or two of them, he may be all right. Then let him come back and settle down at the Works and never go on the road again. It's the only way.' Now, I happened to run across Nehemiah Bibb that very afternoon, and he said that you were through your fourth year, and hadn't any particular church in view— kind o' staying on in Andover, ain't you ?— and he didn't know but you'd like the chance to go around the world.''

" I see,'' said Salem, trying to think fast.

The father watched him keenly. "You'd find Freddie a pleasant fellow to be with," he ventured, persuasively, fancying he saw a refusal upon Salem's face. "And I ought to say this," he continued, "I'll make it worth your while, if you want to go. I know the captain of a brig that sails in August for Australia; expects to touch almost everywhere, either coming or going. How would this do : I to pay all expenses, and two hundred dollars a month, beginning now?"

Kittredge hesitated. It was in many ways the very thing he would like; and the money tempted him, and the opportunity to win back a young man's life. "But we might not get along together," he suggested. "I am three or four years older, and a licensed minister, and——" He could scarcely give an exact phrase to what he felt to be a certain unfitness in the proposed relationship.

"Exactly; you want to go slow and sure. Just like your father. That's all right. But see here : the Richard H. Gulick don't sail till the 16th of August, and to-day's only the 2d of July. Freddie's vacation began yesterday. We're running light at the Works, and his next trip wouldn't be till September anyway. He proposes to go up to Bar Harbor for awhile; thinks the air is better there than it is down on the North Shore where his mother is. Now you go up on the Olivette to-night with him, spend a few weeks together, and get a little acquainted. What do you say?"

" But what would your son say?"

" Oh, that's fixed, nice as you please. I talked it over with him last night; told him all about the way your father and I used to hook off from school together up in Burridge —guess, though, he'd heard me tell that before—and he says, 'All right, send Kittredge along. I've never seen the man yet I couldn't stand if I had to!'"

Salem reflected upon the young man's cordial way of putting it. "I don't know," he said, doubtfully, "suppose we found we couldn't get on smoothly? It must be unpleasant for him to know he is watched. It wouldn't be very agreeable for two men at sword's points to go around the world together."

" To be sure," interrupted Pitman, eagerly, " and that's the beauty of the Bar Harbor idea. Try it for awhile. If it don't work, we won't say anything about the Richard H. Gulick. But I kind o' think it will work, and it does seem as if it was about the only thing there was left to try. There's a good

stiff Maine law, you know ; that might help
you some."

A sense of pity smote Kittredge suddenly.
for the simple - hearted father, for the mother
who did not understand her only boy, for the
boy himself, an inebriate at twenty-three.

" I will undertake it," he said, "and I'll do
my best, but I'm sure I don't know——"

Pitman sprang to his feet. " The Lord bless
you ! Nehemiah Bibb said you would do it.
I'll telephone Freddie that you'll meet him at
the boat to-night. You know where it is—Lewis Wharf. Sails at six, don't she ? Look it
up in that *Globe*." And while Salem picked
up the newspaper, and found the Primitive Pellets staring him in the face again before he
could turn to the steamboat column, Mr. Pitman stepped to a table and wrote a check for
the first six weeks' salary. He would not listen
to Salem's ineffective protest against receiving
it, and they left the Parker House together.
Pitman held up his finger for a herdic, and
shook the younger man's hand with some emotion, looking at his watch meanwhile and giving
directions to the driver. He already had one
foot in the herdic when he turned, and pulled
a big Pellet catalogue from his inside pocket.

" By the way," he said, with a pride not

quite disguised by his offhand tone, "perhaps you'd like to look over one of our new catalogues. It tells all about the Works, and some of those testimonials Freddie got down South are in there. Freddie's picture is on the back page, but he don't know it yet. Good-by!" The herdic disappeared into Washington Street, leaving Salem Kittredge standing on the pavement, his cheeks hot with an embarrassed, unformulated pity, and a colored patent medicine pamphlet in his hand.

II.

THE absurdity of the situation came over him in a moment, and he hurriedly pocketed the catalogue and began to grin. But there was no time to lose in humorous reflection upon his new occupation, if he was to be ready for the Bar Harbor trip that afternoon, and it grew clear to him that the check in his possession was a providential dispensation. Without it, he had barely money enough to get back to Andover; with it, he could purchase a few things that seemed absolutely necessary, if young Pitman were not to be made ashamed of his travelling compan   Exactly what these purchases must be, h   to decide in the course of—it would be hardly accurate to say between the courses of—a forty-five cent dinner at a Brattle Street restaurant.

It was plain that he must procure some clothes, for the black frock suit he had worn into Boston that morning, the only really presentable thing he had, was shiny with the Sunday preaching trips of two winters and a long summer in South Dakota. For the various exigencies of Bar Harbor life, Salem knew that this garb was quite inappropriate. After a miserable hour of indecision, he took the bit in his teeth, and bought a white flannel tennis suit, as something unministerial and sure to be useful. He had a sort of feeling, too, sufficiently definite to make him uncomfortable, that a man going to Mount Desert ought to have a dress-suit, but he was not sure. If young Pitman and he were to start on a voyage around the world in a sailing vessel, a swallow-tail coat would be an impertinence, but the intervening weeks loomed large upon his imagination, and finally, in his honest way, he made a confidant of the salesman who had persuaded him into taking the ready-made tennis suit. The fertile mind of this young gentleman suggested that it might be better to hire evening dress for the time required, and while directing Kittredge to an establishment that made a specialty of such transactions, he assured him that it would be advisable to buy, then and there, whatever else might be needed to complete his evening toilet. The result was that the perplexed theologue gave the salesman permission to pick out what was necessary—a commission which the latter cordially executed, and the affair ended by his escorting Salem to the basement and helping him to select a dress-suit case, extraordinarily heavy and expensive, but absolutely correct in design.

It was with this case in one hand and two big paper parcels in the other—he had telegraphed his Andover landlady to forward his trunk to Mount Desert by express—that Salem walked up the gang-plank of the Olivette shortly after five that afternoon. He was hot and tired and nervous, and the first passenger on board. The purser informed him that a Mr. Pitman had telegraphed for two staterooms, and in one of these Kittredge deposited his belongings. Then, after puzzling over the Spanish notices posted around the cabin—memorials of the winter trips of the little vessel—he went out upon the big covered wharf and sat down upon a box of freight, folding the tails of his frock-coat over into his lap and fanning himself with his black Derby hat, while he kept an eye out for Frederic Pitman.

The Olivette had already taken on most of her freight, but the wharf reverberated with the rolling of hand-trucks and the shouts of the deck-hands as the last consignments were disposed of. Baggage-wagons clattered up to the open side of the building, and deposited piles of trunks, which were checked and put aboard as fast as the owners arrived to identify them. Kittredge kept his seat until he was hustled out of the way by an Italian stevedore, and then he began to walk around among the baggage and wonder whether he could recognize young Pitman when he saw him. The confusion increased momentarily, and amid the throng of clamorous children, jauntily dressed young women, youths in white flannel, jaded mammas, hurrying papas, and Scandinavians and Celts of every condition of servitude, Salem looked in vain for his Confirmed Inebriate. The trunks disappeared gradually within the hold, and the upper deck of the Olivette was filling with passengers. Ten minutes before the time of sailing the wharf was nearly empty once more, and still Salem paced back and forth, pausing to examine the initials upon the late-arriving baggage.

Once his heart beat fast, as he read a big P. upon a steamer trunk, two valises, and a hatbox, and he stepped forward to meet the owner, a stalwart blond fellow in a checked suit and helmet hat. But the dissimilarity between this figure and J. Howard Pitman made him hesitate, and when the stranger, after staring at him an instant, ordered the first officer of the Olivette to book his luggage, it dawned gratefully upon Kittredge that P. might also stand for Plantagenet.

The first officer gravely beckoned to the baggage-master, and continued to converse soothingly with the elder of two ladies, who had been hovering anxiously over the trunks for several minutes. She was a stout little rosy-cheeked personage of fifty-five, and her acute eyes were sparkling behind her gold-rimmed glasses.

"Such an irresponsible system!" she exclaimed.

The first officer shrugged his shoulders.

"Auntie," said the younger woman, "are you quite sure the trunk was not put aboard while I was buying the tickets?"

"Certainly, my child. I was watching every moment. To think that all the plans should be in that particular trunk! Would your deck-hands, sir, dare to put a trunk on board before it had been claimed—while I held the transfer-check in my hand?"

"I should scarcely think so, madam," replied the first officer, who had been summoned from the deck to meet this emergency. "But I will have another search made in the hold at once;" and bowing to the older lady

while looking at the younger one, he shamelessly retreated under fire, leaving Kittredge
and the ladies standing near together.

" It may come yet, Auntie. There are five
minutes left—and then you have the check, in
any case, you know."

" Yes, but, my dear child—— Wait ! We
must telephone the transfer company. Is there
a telephone here ? "

This demand was not addressed to anyone in
particular, but Kittredge glanced toward her as
he heard it, and she made a rapid advance upon
him. " Excuse me," she said, " but possibly
you can help us. Can you tell me if there is a
telephone here ? "

Kittredge glanced vaguely along the floor of
the huge building, down the sides, over to the
Olivette, up to the rafters ; whence his gaze fell
to the sharp bronze feathers of the younger
woman's bonnet, and her fine brown hair, and
the grave blue eyes.

" I—don't see any," he ejaculated. " I'm
very sorry." And then he took off his hat.

" There's a tellyphown in the offus, mum,"
volunteered an interested cabman, with a jerk
of his thumb toward the upper end of the wharf.

" Ah, thank you. Then *will* you please
telephone the transfer company that they must

trace Check 38 instantly, and that we have only five minutes to spare, and that if the trunk does not reach here in time they must express it to me at the Hotel Occidental, at their expense, and that——''

'' Wouldn't it be better to give your name, Auntie ? '' suggested the niece.

'' Of course. Sign it Mrs. Atterbury, please.''

'' Sign it ? '' inquired Kittredge.

'' How very stupid in me ! You know what I mean ! '' exclaimed Mrs. Atterbury, and as the perplexed theologue started on an undignified run for the office, she added to her niece : '' Rachel, I do believe that in my old age I am growing a trifle nervous ! ''

As Salem reached the office door, the clerk in charge was hurrying out to the Olivette.

'' I beg your pardon ; have you a telephone here ? ''

'' Right inside. Help yourself.''

Kittredge groaned. He had counted on getting the clerk to do the talking. It was only once or twice a year that he had occasion to use a telephone, and then he rarely succeeded in making the thing work. But there was not a moment to lose. He laid his hat in a chair, and grasping the handle of the instrument, turned it loud and long. Then he put the receiver to his ear and waited. Outside, there was the hum and rattle of the streets; down the harbor somewhere, a tug-boat was blowing her whistle; out on the wharf there was a scraping sound as if they were hauling up the gang-plank. Salem put the receiver to his other ear, and rang again; but still the mysterious machine was dumb. It occurred to him that perhaps he was expected to speak first.

"Hullo!" His voice was shaky.

"Hullo, Central!" It was slightly louder now, and it seemed to him stentorian.

"Say, Central! Oh-h. Cen-tr-a-l!!" Never had he closed a pulpit discourse with a purer pathos.

Then a cold sweat broke out all over him. He had forgotten to press the button. With a trembling hand he began again, and was greeted with a prompt "Hullo!"

"Is that the Central?"

"Yes."

"Well, I am trying to find Mrs. Atterbury's trunk. It's lost, and she wanted me to telephone to the transfer company——"

"Hold on a minute."

"What did you say?"

"Go ahead. Whom did you wish to call up?"

"The transfer company. I'm trying to find Mrs. Atterbury's trunk, and she wanted me to telephone——"

"Yes, yes. But what number?"

"Number thirty-eight. I think it was a sole-leather trunk, and the Olivette is just starting now, and she says——"

"Wait a minute!" There was a conversation at the other end of the machine, and a confusion of sentences: "Lewis wharf"—"some one there"—"can't make out what he wants"—"no such call as thirty-eight in the book."

Then came a new voice.

"Who is it that's talking?"

"Mr. Kittredge, Salem Kittredge. I am trying to find Mrs. Atterbury's trunk; Misses At-ter-bur-y. She wanted me to telephone to the transfer company——"

"All right. Now hold on. Stand up closer to the telephone. *What transfer company?*"

Salem's heart came up in his throat. He did not have the remotest idea. "I think it was from the Old Colony Depot," he stammered desperately. "But it may have been the Albany Depot, or perhaps it was the New England. Can't you try them all?" he went on, penitently but hopelessly. "The fact is, she didn't tell me, and——"

There was a quick rustle of skirts behind him, and Kittredge turned. In the narrow doorway of the dingy office stood Rachel Atterbury, slender, alert as a bird just alighting, one gray-gloved hand resting on the doorjamb and the other supported by the handle of her parasol. She leaned toward him, a flush of color in her cheeks, her lips parted with her quick breathing.

"Auntie's trunk is found!" she panted. "It was in the hold all the time! We were so afraid you would be left. It was so very kind of you to take this trouble."

Salem stared at her an instant in abject, speechless gratitude; then he let the telephone receiver swing dangling back against the wall and stammered, with admirable sincerity, "You're welcome. You are very welcome."

They hurried toward the Olivette side by side. The deck-hands had already laid hold of the ropes of the gang-plank, and the boat was quivering with the slow turning of her screw. Frederic Pitman had gone utterly out of Kittredge's mind. But as they reached the boat, they encountered a spectacle which recalled to the theologue the aim of his excursion to Mount Desert. A red-faced, pot-bellied hackman bore down upon them, staggering under the weight of a huge, commercial traveller's trunk; and in the rear of this combination appeared the Confirmed Inebriate, a smallish young man with a pert nose and demure eyes, immaculately dressed in blue serge, russet shoes, and yachting cap, carrying his head thrown forward, his elbows very slightly outward, and his knees very daintily bent as he walked, and with a bundle of silver - headed sticks and umbrellas in his hand. It was with this bundle that he politely touched the hackman's elbow, and indicated where the trunk should be thrown on board; then he caught sight of Miss Atterbury. She recognized him, with a somewhat formal inclination, and passed swiftly up the plank. His lips murmured her name respectfully; his bow was the perfection of good form.

"This is Mr. Pitman?" said Kittredge, wondering how Mrs. Atterbury's niece could happen to know an inebriate, but feeling instinctively sure of his man.

"Yes; Mr. Kittredge, I believe? I am very glad to meet you. After you."

And in that order they mounted to the deck of the Olivette.

III.

THE experience of Salem Kittredge as a student of theology, and even as a frontier preacher for a space of some four months, had scarcely accustomed him to such prompt action and swift transitions as had marked that afternoon. It was difficult for him to keep more than one thing in his head at a time, and from the moment the Atterbury ladies had appealed to him in their anxiety until he spied his Inebriate, he had quite forgotten the real reason of his journey to Bar Harbor. But his memory was sharply jogged before he had been a minute upon the deck of the steamer. Young Mr. Pitman excused himself in order to look up his state-room, leaving Kittredge leaning over the rail of the boat watching her work her way out of the slip. The quartermaster was close beside him, lowering a rope buffer between the steamer and the black piles of the wharf, and conversing respectfully with the second officer.

" D' ye remember that little feller who just come aboard ? "

" No. I don't know as I do," replied the second officer.

" Why, he was that feller that wanted to charter the Olivette to carry a cargo of pills from Tampa to Havana, last winter."

" Is that so ? Well, he was lively for a little one, wa'n't he ? "

" I guess he was ! " And, bending still farther over, he swung the buffer just in time to catch the whole weight of the straining boat, and as it creaked and flattened with the pressure, he added, judicially : " There ain't any bichloride of gold in *his* blood ! "

Salem turned away, with a sudden sinking at his heart. He was there to watch over a drunkard ; such was the service to which he owed his salary ; he had drawn that salary in advance, and he must earn it somehow. Restlessly he made his way to the upper deck, and there ran across Mrs. Atterbury, who had thriftily taken possession of a chair and had scattered her wraps over two or three others. She scrutinized him through the gold-rimmed eye-glasses an instant, and then stopped him as he was passing her.

" You must let me thank you for your kindness," she said, in a clear, rapid voice. " It was very obliging of you to telephone for me. I have no doubt it did some good, even if those stupid porters had put the trunk aboard already. You see the company ought to be reprimanded constantly for its carelessness, on general principles. I am glad they had a man to talk to them. But we feared the boat might start without you ; we were very grateful."

" Oh, I—I really did very little," said Kittredge, blushing.

" That is for us to decide," graciously replied Mrs. Atterbury, " and no one knows how much good it may have done the transfer company."

The theologue had the appearance of deferentially waiving this question, but he could not think of anything to say, and the pause in the conversation indicated that his brief acquaintance with Mrs. Atterbury had already reached its limit. As he hesitated, on the point of leaving her, the Inebriate brushed past his elbow, and was greeted by the lady with a smile of recognition and an outstretched hand.

" Why, how do you do, Mr. Pitman ! I remember meeting you at Magnolia. Is your mother on board ? "

" Mother is not here," responded Mr. Pitman, with a slightly husky voice, into which he succeeded in pouring a most unctuous regret, and with a look of bland resignation in his brown eyes. " Mother has felt obliged to remain in Magnolia this summer. It would have given her great pleasure to meet you again. I see you know Mr. Kittredge," he added, turning to Salem.

" Yes, indeed ! Mr. Kittredge has been of the greatest service to us ; he must have telephoned all over the city in search of a trunk that contained the plans for our cottage. We couldn't have lost it, you know. Tell me, Mr. Pitman, is not a transfer company liable under the circumstances to the full extent of the law ? "

The Inebriate nodded gravely.

" Won't you take these chairs ? " she went on. " It will be impossible to find one in a few minutes, the boat is so crowded ; " and with hospitable zeal she piled her travelling-rugs upon the deck and insisted that the young men should sit down. The fleet Olivette had already left the docks far behind her and was headed down the channel. Young Pitman and Mrs. Atterbury were still deep in the discussion of the trunk question — broken by occasional comments upon the speed of the steamer or the familiar beauty of the harbor — when Salem caught sight of Rachel Atterbury picking her way toward them through the crowded chairs. She had exchanged the bronze-feathered bonnet for a blue Tam O'Shanter, and the collar of her tight-fitting jacket was turned up around her throat, making her figure seem even slenderer than before. Just as she reached the group, the wash from a passing schooner struck the Olivette's quarter; and the girl, with a little gasp, threw up her hands to balance herself, and was poised for a single instant in the very attitude in which she had appeared to Salem at the dingy office door upon the wharf. He sprang to his feet, followed by the Inebriate.

"My niece, Miss Atterbury—Mr. Pitman. Oh, of course! You have met at Magnolia; I should have remembered it. And Mr. Kittredge."

Again Salem noticed that her bow to Frederic Pitman, though perfectly pleasant, was formal, far more so than her recognition of himself; and of the chairs which the two gentlemen offered her, she accepted Kittredge's. A keen sense of pleasure thrilled him. He talked eagerly, gayly, cutting short her reiteration of gratitude about that wretched telephone; and young Pitman, glancing shrewdly at them in the pauses of his own conversation with the aunt, decided that his new companion was more of a ladies' man than he looked.

When the steamer had made the Light, and was headed away for the darkening northeast, the cooler wind and increasing motion drove most of the passengers from the upper deck. But in the west there was a gorgeous sunset, and off the port quarter the flash of first one and then another distant light, and the Atterbury ladies, wrapped in their rugs, sat watching it all until the dusk fell close around the sharp black bow of the Olivette, and there was a scent in the air like that of a coming fog. Then they went down to supper, leaving the two young men, for the first time, alone together.

Salem felt that the moment had come for them to reach an understanding of the peculiar relation into which they were about to enter ; and Freddie Pitman seemed to realize his companion's thought, for he turned up the collar of his overcoat, stretched his feet irreverently upon the chair which Miss Atterbury had abandoned, and sat eying Kittredge as if waiting for him to begin. But it was exceedingly difficult for the theologue to invent an introduction to his discourse, and he had a decidedly vague idea of what the discourse itself ought to be.

"Well," he said, "here we are."

"Yes," assented Pitman, politely, "here we are." The fact, indeed, was indubitable. Salem was shaking with the cold, and dizzy with the rise and fall of the steamer's bow.

"I suppose," he ventured, "we ought to have something of a talk."

"Yes?" was the response. "What do you say to a smoke?" Freddie Pitman unbuttoned his coat and held out a plethoric cigar-case.

"No, I thank you," said Salem, hurriedly, his teeth chattering as he spoke, and the bare idea of smoking or seeing anyone else smoke seemed suddenly to augment by ten or fifteen degrees that upward and downward pitch of the bow.

"Look here, aren't you cold? Hadn't you better get your overcoat?"

"I—I left it in Andover. I *am* a little cold. Perhaps I ought to eat some supper," he added, weakly, as he caught the first whiff of Pitman's cigar.

"Of course. That will make you feel better—warmer, I mean"—he corrected himself instantly—"and I will wait here for you if you like. I had a five o'clock dinner, and nearly lost the boat by it, so I think I won't go down."

Salem rose unsteadily and made his way aft, while the wind lifted his shiny coat-tails and forced him to keep tight hold of his stiff hat. Down the companion-way he stumbled, and into the dining-saloon, but a single look at the tables convinced him that supper was not what he needed. Slowly, dizzily, he dragged himself to the fresh air of the upper deck once more, and stood there a moment watching the red tip of Pitman's cigar, as the young fellow paced nonchalantly back and forth upon the deserted deck ; but just then the tricky Olivette began to roll a little, Freddie Pitman's cigar-tip seemed to circle up—up—up, and to whirl down—down—down, and Salem Kittredge suddenly remembered that he had a state-room.

Two hours later there was a gentle knock at that state-room door, and Pitman entered quietly. The theologue was stretched face downward in his berth, his coat off, shivering, but too wretched to stir.

" Hullo ! " said Freddie, " I've been wondering where you were. Couldn't imagine what had become of you. But it's sensible to turn in early ; this looks like a bad night, and I'm going to follow suit. Allow me, Mr. Kittredge, it will make you more comfortable." As he spoke, he covered Salem dexterously with the blankets from both berths. "Nonsense, let me pull your shoes off—there! And now, my dear fellow, your teeth are chattering so that I can't go to sleep in the next state-room. You must let me prescribe; wait a second—here, swallow this; no, I'll hold it; don't try to sit up; just open your mouth and shut your eyes—so-o—there!"

But when Salem had stopped choking, and the fiery liquid had begun to diffuse a delicious warmth throughout his vitals, he opened his eyes sufficiently to behold a friendly and extraordinarily infectious smile upon the features of the Inebriate, who was carefully screwing down the top of a brandy-flask.

IV.

AT five the next morning the Olivette
changed her course and slackened speed,
cautiously feeling her way in the fog toward a
certain bell-buoy. The altered rhythm of her
engines woke Kittredge from a sleep which even
the Olivette's fog-whistle, blowing for the past
two hours, had not disturbed. He raised himself upon one elbow and stared sleepily around
the state-room. There were his new dress-suit
case and the paper parcels, just as he had left
them; but his long black coat, which he indis-
tinctly remembered dropping upon the floor, was
now suspended neatly from a hook, and his shoes
were placed carefully beneath it. His shoes?
He recalled that when he went to bed he had
decided, all at once, not to take off his shoes.
Gracious! There flashed over him the quiet
kindness of Pitman — and the blankets — and
that scorching spirituous draught. He flung
himself out of the berth and looked in the
mirror. His eyes were not bloodshot, nor were

his features haggard ; his hair was mussed, certainly, but his head was clear as a bell ; he glanced out of the port-hole at the glassy water and the luminous fog through which the boat seemed scarcely more than drifting ; then he counted his pulse, and decided he had never felt better in his life.

In half an hour he had bathed, arrayed himself, after some hesitation, in his new white suit, and was knocking at Pitman's state-room. As there was no answer, and the door was slightly ajar, Kittredge thrust his head in, and beheld the Inebriate slumbering peacefully in the lower berth. For a moment Salem watched him. It was a very young face, and scarcely seemed a bad one ; the collar of the silk night-robe was drawn close up to the chin, whose lines were delicate and almost firm ; the mouth was winning, the saucy nose lent a certain gayness to the countenance, the brown hair was tumbled in boyish fashion ; and while Kittredge was still looking, the demure eyes opened wide and smiled a morning greeting.

" How do you do ? " said Salem ; " I thought I'd see if you were awake."

" That's all right. Come in. What time is it ? "

" It's moving along toward six," replied

Kittredge, "and I didn't know but we should be getting in soon."

"Exactly," yawned Pitman, directing his brown eyes inquiringly at the theologue's flannel suit. But he made no comment, and announced an intention of arising in a very few minutes and annihilating the Olivette's fog-whistle. In this work of destruction Salem was cordially invited to join, and he assented to the extent of agreeing to wait for Pitman upon the upper deck, that they might begin operations together. Thither, accordingly, Salem betook himself, fairly satisfied with the pleasantry he had exchanged with his *protégé*, and feeling himself to be a quite different person from the man who had retreated down those slippery saloon stairs the night before.

The morning was delicious. The Olivette was still enwrapped with fog, so thick that with a double lookout at the bow, she did not dare to steam ahead at full speed ; yet in her wake it was all translucent in the sun, gleaming with a hundred tints of mother-of-pearl and clouded opal, and around her keel it slowly rose like drifting smoke from the dull-green water. Kittredge threw back his shoulders, and took a deep breath of the salt air. Then he observed Miss Atterbury, who was leaning over the rail

to watch a floating jelly-fish, and in the buoy-
ancy of that moment he stepped promptly to
her side. She started as she caught sight of his
big hand upon the rail, so close to her own,
and for an instant she failed to recognize him
in his utterly changed attire.

" Good - morning ! " he exclaimed. " Did
you sleep well ? "

"Oh, good-morning, Mr.—Mr. Kittredge,"
she said, straightening up. " I beg your pardon ? "

" Did the fog-whistle keep you awake ? "
He beamed at her with benevolent gray eyes.

" Yes, indeed, for the longest time. Was it
not dreadful ? "

" Well, I didn't hear it myself," he admitted. " I must have been very sound asleep.
But Mr. Pitman says that it was the—that it
was very annoying. He proposes to smash it
when he comes up, and wants me to help him."

" Ah ? Mr. Pitman must be very vindic-
tive," she said, smilingly. " Don't you think
one ought to be more forgiving on a perfect
morning like this ? "

" I ? Oh, I could forgive anything or anybody to-day, I am sure. And perhaps Mr.
Pitman didn't mean it. I don't know him
very well."

" No ? "

" No, not really. In fact, I met him only yesterday. You see I have been a theological student, and——"

He hesitated, and she helped him out a little, in feminine fashion.

" Yes, I think you told me you had been studying at Andover. What a lovely old place Andover is, isn't it ? "

" You have been there, then ? "

" I have only driven through, with Auntie and a coaching party. But I interrupted you, did I not ? "

" No," he said, bluntly, his feeling of loyalty to the young fellow keeping him from the explanation he had started to give, " Pitman and I are just travelling together."

She nodded silently, looking him in the eyes. Kittredge remembered her coolness toward Pitman the night before, and was sure she had guessed the relationship between himself and the Inebriate. But she changed the subject. " I was just watching the funniest jelly-fish ! " she remarked, looking down at the water again. " I wonder if you can tell me its name ; there were so many of them here a few moments ago. Do you study jelly-fishes at the theological seminary, Mr. Kittredge ? "

"No," he replied; "we have them there, but we don't study them, except incidentally."

She glanced at him with a delightful smile of comprehension. "I have met some of the men in our own theological school at Cambridge, and—yes, they are queer. But many of them are very nice—really, not jelly-fishy at all."

"I don't suppose we can help it—to a certain extent," said Kittredge, fearing that he had slandered his brethren, and at the same time offering a guilty apology for himself; "it's the nature of the life we lead—the defect of our qualities, if you like."

"No," she insisted, "I don't admit it. The Church—the ministry, I mean—is a noble profession; it is quite the noblest. And some of the men are charming. We have had several of them in some informal dances this last winter; they were so clever, too."

"Indeed? I am afraid we are not all clever at Andover. But we have some sterling men."

She interrupted him, pointing eagerly down to the water. "Quick!" she cried, "isn't it a nautilus? A real Chambered Nautilus?"

Kittredge looked critically at the tiny floating object. "I'm sure I don't know. Is he sailing away from his low-vaulted past or does he take it with him?"

"Oh, he leaves it behind!" she laughed. "Don't you remember? 'Leave thy low-vaulted past'—it comes just after 'Build thou more stately mansions, O my soul.' That last is the line I've been teasing Auntie with all the spring. I maintain that her house at Newton, built by old Colonel Atterbury himself, is ever so much nicer than this new cottage at Bar Harbor. Did she offer to show you the plans?"

"No," said Kittredge, "but I believe she discussed them with Mr. Pitman."

"Those plans are a perfect mania with Auntie; you should hear her talk them over with the coachman! If the trunk had veritably been lost, Mr. Kittredge, I'm sure I can't imagine what we should have done. The architect has just sailed for Europe. Auntie will never forget your kindness, but I am certain that you cannot escape looking over the plans."

"But I shall enjoy it!" he exclaimed. "I think house-building is very delightful. And until it is finished?"

"We shall remain at the Occidental."

The theologue flushed with pleasure. "We are going there too!" he cried. "Perhaps you will let me—let us—see something of you?"

The thought of the Inebriate made him hesitate ; he wondered whether he should find himself under a social ban because of his companion, and he had an uncomfortable minute or two while he pretended to watch the nautilus drift away into the lifting fog.

"I do not really know Mr. Pitman," she began, after a little, as if she were thinking of the very same thing as Kittredge. "I heard some talk about him at Magnolia last summer. His father is the patent-medicine man, is he not?"

Salem nodded with a queer expression in his face. "'Si monumentum quæris,'" said he, "just look at that!"

The fog had been swept apart by a sudden breeze, and all around there were tiny islands, covered with thick clumps of spruce, where blue jays and crows were calling to each other. On a huge bowlder just off the bow of the Olivette, still glistening from the falling tide, was the following legend, in white letters upon an azure field: *Use Pitman's Primitive Pellets.*

"What horrid vandalism!" she cried, indignantly. "Should you not think that——"

Salem heard a step behind them, and turning, hurriedly touched her arm. She smothered an exclamation and faced around, a charming color in her cheeks. The Inebriate advanced unconsciously, his mouth quirked into the most agreeable of smiles. Kittredge tried to throw his broad shoulders˙ between Pitman and that staring sign, but it was Miss Atterbury who saved the day.

" Mr. Pitman," she said, " we've been talking of your threatened assault upon the steamwhistle, and I don't even know where the thing is. Won't you please show me ? "

The flattered Inebriate extended his elbow with a bow. She took his arm instantly, and off they marched, with their backs turned upon the bowlder and Mr. Kittredge, who stood there somewhat vacantly by the rail. Miss Atterbury and her companion were in perfect step, and she kept turning cosily toward him as they promenaded, but Salem could not help thinking that she was quite too tall for his *protégé*. Possibly Mrs. Atterbury, who joined Kittredge at the instant when his reflections upon this point were in danger of growing a trifle sombre, may have shared his feeling that there was a certain incongruity in that sudden friendliness, for she lifted her eye-glasses and regarded her niece steadily, while Kittredge murmured something about getting Pitman away from a Pellet advertisement that might have been awkward for him.

"For him?" laughed the widow. "Scarcely; I fancy he is not easily embarrassed; but for my niece and yourself, very possibly. And you were really just looking at it when he came up!" She laughed again; a light, resonant laugh for a woman of fifty-five. "But my niece can make up her mind very quickly on occasion, Mr. Kittredge. She can extricate herself, when necessary, as well as most people."

"I should judge so," said the theologue, with as much admiration as he dared express. "She tells me you are going to build here."

"Yes, the revised plans were in that trunk you so kindly traced for us yesterday. You must let me show them to you some day."

"Certainly," assented Kittredge promptly. "I shall be most pleased."

"Very good; perhaps you will be the one to assure me whether my architect has made a triumph of the stairs. No one seems sufficiently positive about it. We shall be at the Occidental," she added.

"I am to be there too!" Salem exclaimed; "that is—Mr. Pitman and myself."

"Oh!" said Mrs. Atterbury, slowly.

And just then the Olivette leaped forward under full pressure of her steam, glided past the vessels of the White Squadron lying lazily at anchor in the channel, and in five minutes was made fast to the little wooden wharf at Bar Harbor. Salem took one comprehensive glance at the flotilla of Indian canoes and steam yachts, the crowd of truckmen and hotel-runners on the wharf, the Club House and the big hotels looming through the mist; then he started for his state-room in search of the two brown paper parcels and his dress-suit case.

Upon the saloon stairs he met Miss Atterbury. She was hastening up to the deck, buttoning her gloves as she went, but she stopped Salem as they were passing each other.

"Could he have heard?" she whispered, her eyes looking straight into his. "I was never so frightened in my life. Do you think he heard?"

"I hardly think so. You were very quick-witted; and, if you will allow me," he added, bluntly, "you made him ample amends, even if he did hear." He was jealous of the way she had taken the Inebriate's arm.

Miss Atterbury fastened her last glove-button deliberately; then she raised her eyebrows ever so slightly, and made him a mock courtesy. "Yes?" she said, and the crowd upon the stairs swept them apart.

43

V.

THE Saturday-night hops at the Occidental were one of the leading features of that admirably conducted hotel. They were not so exclusive as the affairs at the Pelican, nor were they by any means so democratic as the dances at Pibroch's; a delightful informality prevailed, and yet a great many people from the Cuttyhunk and the Pelican and the cottages were sure to be there. The tiny orchestra played in excellent time, and the ball-room floor was reputed to be the best in Bar Harbor. Long French windows opened directly from the ball-room upon the immense veranda, where hundreds of people could promenade at once, or sit in cosey groups before the windows to watch the dancing. The gentlemen who ran down to Mount Desert to spend Sunday with their families usually preferred to lean against the piazza railing and enjoy a tranquil cigar rather than to make themselves useful to their wives and daughters upon the floor; and yet, after all deductions, there was always a greater

44

number of available men at the Occidental than anywhere else on the island.

Salem Kittredge was hardly an available man, inasmuch as he had never danced in his life ; but nevertheless, upon the first Saturday night after his arrival he appeared extremely early at the ball-room, in evening dress. Why he was there he scarcely knew. He had had several wretched days. On reaching the hotel a telegram from J. Howard Pitman had been handed him : " Have just seen the doctor. Says this is the week to watch him. Look out. God bless you." Was the crucial test coming, before they were even acquainted ? Salem would have flung up his commission in dismay, had it not been for the fact that he had already spent part of the salary, and for the " God bless you " on the end of the despatch. He tried to have a frank talk with his *protégé*, but although Freddie Pitman accepted the situation with the utmost amiability, he absolutely refused to discuss it.

" We'll stick together, Kittie," he declared —he had dubbed his companion Kittie in the course of the first forenoon—" and you can keep your eye on me as much as you please. That's what J. Howard is paying the bills for, and much good may it do us all. But if I have any little eccentricities of my own, they are my own. Do you see?"

Salem saw with great distinctness, and the subject was dropped. But all day long, for four days, the young men kept together. They lounged upon the broad veranda, or played feebly at tennis. They drove to Spouting Horn, and paddled a canoe over to Porcupine Island. Hour after hour did they walk around a billiard-table in a dingy second-floor room on the main street of the village, while the Inebriate gave Kittredge forty points in a fifty-point game and invariably beat him. Side by side did they do ravage upon the well-known cuisine of the Occidental, and vainly tried to bribe the head-waiter to give them one of the cool little tables by the window, where the Atterburys were always seated ; and nothing occurred to mar the polished surface of young Pitman's good nature, or to relieve the wretched anxiety that preyed upon Kittredge's mind. He had so little to go by; he wished he had asked the Pellet man to send the doctor's detailed statement of the phenomena of the " convulsive form of acute alcoholism," or whatever the thing was called, which he might expect at at any moment. He made sure, by a shamefaced examination of Pitman's belongings, that there were no intoxicants there. Even the travelling flask was empty, and that, as Salem ruefully reflected, had very possibly been emptied by himself.

He remembered what J. Howard Pitman had remarked about the Maine law, and one day, with some embarrassment, he asked the livery agent who always hung about the door of the Occidental whether there was any place at Bar Harbor where liquor was sold. The agent looked sharply at him from under the visor of his cap.

"No," he said, "there ain't. And yet," he added, in a lower voice and with something of a twinkle, "if all you want is a drink, I can set right here on this stoop, 'n point you out seventeen places, not counting drug-stores and hotels, where you can git it. But what's the matter with right here at the Occidental?"

Salem shrugged his shoulders, with as much duplicity as he could muster, and laughed the question off. But his heart sank.

It was only at night, after young Pitman had turned out the gas in the inner of the adjoining rooms that constituted No. 37, and called "Good-night, Kittie!" that Salem had any peace of mind. Then he used to stretch himself comfortably in his own bed, and for a season forget the Inebriate in meditation upon other subjects. There, for instance, was Miss Atterbury. Kittredge had seen but little of his acquaintances of the Olivette. True to her promise, Mrs. Atterbury had brought down the plans for the cottage and had exhibited them to him one morning upon a sheltered corner of the piazza ; but what with keeping one eye conscientiously on Freddie Pitman, and the other, quite unconsciously, on Miss Rachel, who was promenading back and forth with the stalwart Englishman he had noticed in Boston, Kittredge did not win any peculiar credit as a critic of domestic architecture. He could trace the twinkling of Miss Atterbury's russet Oxford ties down that immense veranda far more accurately than the course of Mrs. Atterbury's marvellous winding staircase. Even after that young woman had dismissed her British admirer, and, rejoining her aunt, had pointed out with her own finger the music-room and the loggia and the butler's pantry, Kittredge praised the blue sheets confusedly, though at that moment it could not even be urged in his excuse that one eye was directed to Frederic Pitman. It was after Mrs. Atterbury had rolled up the plans, in some politely disguised disappointment at Salem's perceptive faculties, that

Miss Atterbury made an observation about the hops at the Occidental. The season before they had been very delightful, she said; the men almost always dressed for them; it was very good of the men to take the trouble to dress; did not Mr. Kittredge think so?

Salem quoted this remark with some impressiveness to Pitman, after dinner on Saturday evening, when they were both in No. 37.

" Is that so? " said the Inebriate, looking up from a novel by Gaboriau. " I imagined those things were informal. Over at the Pelican, you know, you ought to dress for dinner; that's why I didn't go there. Nevertheless, I suppose one might please the dear creatures once a week. Make your toilet, Kittie; go ahead; I want to finish this first, and I've got to shave besides, so don't wait. I'll be there to see you home, my dear."

Several times during the next half-hour did Pitman glance through the door at the theologue, who was brushing the wrinkles out of his rented coat, nervously inserting shirt-studs, and examining his tie despondently in the mirror. Finally he hesitated in Lapham-like wretchedness over the problem of gloves, and Freddie shut his novel and lounged into the other room.

" Going down? " he commented, carelessly.

" Look here, I don't propose to wear gloves unless I have to dance, and perhaps not then. You'd better back me up."

" Oh, all right," assented Kittredge, with a promptness that repaid Pitman for his effort. " Just as you say."

Pitman surveyed him critically. " You're as fresh as a rose-bud, Kittie. And that reminds me I ought to have ordered a bouquet for you. I wish I had your color ! Plain living and high thinking, eh ? Au revoir ! "

Salem went down for once in the elevator, to the edification of the boy, and lingered awkwardly a moment at the ball-room door. The orchestra was playing, and some little girls were practising polka steps over in one corner. A few matrons decorated the benches at the sides. Kittredge took a full breath, put his new dress shoes very cautiously upon the waxed floor, and steered obliquely across the room and out upon the piazza, while the matrons examined him interestedly and the little girls thought that now surely the hop was going to begin. Salem leaned against the window-casing ; his face had all the vacancy of a professional leader of germans ; but the hop did not begin. By and by he dropped into a big rocking-chair outside. He was profoundly uncomfortable. He wished

Pitman would come; he wished that he smoked, so that he might give himself at least a nonchalant air; he wished that he could walk up and down the veranda, but there was no one to walk with, and he felt that his full dress made him too conspicuous to walk alone. Now and then a bevy of young girls came waltzing down the corridor from the card-rooms, circled the big floor, and whirled back again. A few extemporized couples stepped in from the piazza, danced a few rounds, and were once more lost in the groups of on-lookers.

But gradually it began to seem more like a hop. Two or three indefatigable youths in tennis suits and sashes were taking every dance. Young women glided in from nowhere in particular; and when a party came over from the Pelican—all of the men in irreproachable toilet, and one with a cravat of exactly the same extreme style as his own—Kittredge commenced to feel not so much out of place after all. His great mistake, he reflected, had been in coming down so early. He still sat there in his rocker, and waited, in a vague way, for Miss Atterbury. He had a sort of instinct that they would drift together, and that she would be pleased to see him in evening dress. He could not dance with her, he did not even hope to walk with her, and yet he felt sure that they would meet. An hour passed. At last she came; Salem recognized her the instant she emerged from the office door with her aunt. They paused a moment, looking down the veranda; then they advanced slowly, the girl in front, threading her way among the crowded chairs close by the railing, where the breeze blew the hanging Virginia creeper against her shoulders, and the electric lamps, blended with the moonlight, shone full upon her face. People turned to look at her as she went by. She passed the first window and then the second; Salem was waiting by the third. He sprang up eagerly as the ladies reached it.

" Good-evening ! " he exclaimed. " I have been hoping for you. Mrs. Atterbury, take this chair. Miss Atterbury, allow me." But the aunt saw an old acquaintance just inside the ball-room, and would not sit down.

" Rachel may stay if she likes," she graciously permitted. " Don't catch cold, my dear; take this wrap. Thank you, Mr. Kittredge."

The girl leaned forward in her chair, and Kittredge dropped the soft wool wrap around her shoulders. Her gown was a delicate blue gauze, and she drew the wrap tightly about her as she sat back again and looked up at him. He was finer-looking than she had thought : clear-eyed, dark-haired, with a fresh color in his honest face ; as cleanly-built, wholesome a fellow of twenty-six as Bar Harbor could exhibit. She was pleased to think that someone had been planning for her coming—a young woman of twenty-five knows that the time may arrive when these small attentions will be held at their due price—and she resolved to be very nice to him.

They talked of the breeze, the White Squadron, and the house plans ; of the people from the Pelican, now thick upon the ball-room floor, and of the fabulous *table d'hôte* at the Cuttyhunk ; they discussed their personal likes and dislikes, the perils of American democracy, and the spread of ritualism in the Episcopal Church ; and still he did not ask her to dance. She wondered if he knew how. She had not supposed him a dancing man, but his full dress puzzled her ; she had not the remotest idea that he had acted upon her chance remark about the gentlemen of the previous season. He was talking well, and she was conscious of liking him, of really liking him very much, and yet she was dying to dance ; it was a delicious waltz the orchestra was playing—one of Delibes's things. She glanced occasionally at the Honourable Plantagenet, as he circled past the window in a gorgeous waistcoat. He would ask her, she knew.

Yet she made Salem feel that she utterly ignored what was going on in the ball-room. He would have sworn that one could not converse so earnestly about ritualism with a mind inclined at the same moment to a mundane pleasure. Her grave blue eyes did not seem for an instant to be wandering from his own. He was perfectly at his ease now ; he was in fairyland.

It was one of those ardent youths in white flannel, who had been whispering together and looking toward Miss Atterbury, that finally broke the spell, for he crossed to the threshold where she was sitting, and made her his best dancing-school bow. The music was just beginning again. " Good-evening, Richard," she said, smilingly; "are you sure you are not too tired ? " And with a deprecating glance at Kittredge, as if to say, " You see I do not wish to disappoint the boy," she glided off. It took Salem a minute to realize the situation : a boy had carried her away from him, an accursed boy with grass-stains on his tennis trousers and a rent in his rumpled sash !

He rose helplessly to his feet. Someone

touched his elbow; it was the little fellow who ran the elevator. "The clerk wants to see you in the office, sir," he whispered. Salem groaned. He had forgotten Pitman for two whole hours, and hurriedly he shouldered his way up the veranda to the office, with a certainty that something was wrong.

The clerk leaned over the desk confidentially. "The head-waiter says he has had to send a good deal of liquid up to 37 to-night. Can you keep that young fellow quiet?" Kittredge dashed up the two flights and down the corridor to the door of No. 37. He listened a moment; the Inebriate's husky tenor was meandering gently through the second stanza of Bishop Heber's missionary hymn. He entered firmly. Upon the centre-table, flanked by a little pitcher of shaving water and the glasses from both dressing-tables, stood a beautiful illustration of the working of the Maine law, while in front of Salem's mirror was Freddie Pitman in his shirt-sleeves. He was trying to shave, but his hand was no steadier than his voice, and he wiped the bloody lather from his razor onto the back cover of the Gaboriau novel, as he turned to greet Kittredge with an oath.

55

VI

A T ten o'clock Sunday morning Kittredge, who had shortly before dawn flung himself upon his bed without undressing, was wakened by a familiar voice. He opened his eyes with a nervous start, stared a moment at his disordered evening dress, and then at Freddie Pitman, who was perched in dishabille upon the foot of the bed. The Inebriate's pert little face was rather white and preternaturally serious.

"Kittie," he began, "you tell me about last night, will you?" Salem shook his head, as if to get rid of a memory.

"Look here," continued Pitman, "it may not be very pleasant for you, and it isn't so peculiarly pleasant for me, but I want to know just what happened. You came in while I was shaving, didn't you?"

Kittredge nodded.

"Well, I'll shave the other side by and by. You can give the bell-boy a quarter to go around and pick up that razor. It's too good a one to throw out the window. You must have been a trifle nervous at that stage of the game, Kittie.''

The Inebriate himself was certainly cool enough at present. ''And then, let me see,'' he continued ; ''no, before that you threw out some other articles, didn't you? Yes; well, you needn't say anything to the bell-boy about that. And then you locked the door and tipped your chair back against it, confound you—I mean bless you—and that's about as far as I can get.''

'' That's far enough,'' said Salem, raising himself upon one elbow.

'' No, it isn't,'' persisted Freddie. '' I'll tell you pretty soon why I want to know. I suppose I—used some strong expressions ? ''

'' Tolerably.''

'' Pernicious effect of early education. I take them all back, Kittie. Did I show fight ? ''

'' Rather.''

'' Well, I was outclassed, wasn't I ? I got the feather-weight sparring out at Cambridge, but I guess I wasn't in it with you.''

'' I began to think, once, that you were.'' It was when the razor had gone out of the window.

'' Thank you,'' said Pitman, appreciatively ;

and then he lowered his voice, and there was an uneasy curiosity in his eyes. " Did I roll on the floor much ? "

Kittredge sat up straight, and smoothed out the wrinkles in his shirt-bosom before replying : " I don't see why you should want to go into these details, Pitman."

" Exactly. I don't want to, Kittie ; but if the symptoms aren't improving the doctor tells me I'm a gone case—done for. You grasp it, I suppose ? Now answer me four questions— it's for the doctor, you know—and I'll let you off."

Kittredge shuddered a little, as one image after another—pitiful, horrible, grotesque—rose afresh before his eyes ; but he answered the questions, whereupon Freddie sprang to his feet with a delighted cry.

" Better ! Every one of them better ! Kittie, if man, woman, or dog would stand by me when this thing comes on, I could beat it ! I know it. You see, the interval was five days longer than before. Will you believe me if I tell you something ? " He scrambled up nearer to Kittredge and put out his hand. " For seven weeks, if we stay together, you needn't worry about me at all. I won't want a drop of anything. I never take a nip at my

own travelling-flask, even. I'm a regular Tem-
perance Band, all by my little self. But the
eighth or ninth week, look out; don't leave
me, man, will you? I didn't intend to fool
you last night; I honestly meant to come
downstairs, but symptom No. 1 struck me and
I couldn't help myself. If someone would
stick right by me then, I'd be all solid in two
years more. The doctor said so. And," he
added, with a queer quavering smile, " I'm
blessed if I'm not worth saving, if I do say
it."

Kittredge wrung his hand. For the first
time since he met the Inebriate he felt heart-
certain that the young fellow was honest with
him. And then Pitman shivered.

" I'm going back to bed; I'll sleep till
dinner-time ; two-thirty, you know, Sundays.
You must have caught cold, man, lying there
just before that window. You'd better take a
hot bath right away and get some breakfast.
Good-by ! "

Church-bells were ringing somewhere as he
closed the door. Kittredge lay a moment
with his eyes shut, listening to them, before
getting up. He had been right, after all, he
thought, in coming to Bar Harbor. Then,
with joints stiff from the chilly fog that had all

night overwrapped the village and still clung
about the bare summit of Green Mountain, he
rose, and followed Pitman's advice about the
bath and breakfast.

Three-quarters of an hour afterward he left
the hotel and blundered by mistake into the
Chapel of St. Anastasia. The usher set a chair
in the aisle for him, and as he had come in so
late, he did not wish to withdraw, though he
felt no particular interest in the unimpeachable
platitudes about " The Moral Uses of Courtesy,"
which a great bishop was delivering. In the
course of his brief frontier experience, Salem
had written too many poor sermons himself not
to know one when he heard it, and his eyes
wandered. He had never seen so many perfectly dressed people in his life, and they all
seemed listening devoutly. Doors and windows
were wide open, and a breeze from the pine
forests crept through the chapel, soothing every
sense to a delicious calm. He wondered if he
should go to sleep if he closed his eyelids a
little—ever so little—they felt so hot. He
found himself nodding once, twice, then with
a virtuous effort he sat bolt upright, and from
this vantage ground discovered Rachel Atterbury's bonnet.

It was directly in front of one of the open

windows, and he had the absurd fancy that the blue-winged lace might fly out at any instant if he did not watch. He bent forward a trifle; no, it was fastened by velvet ribbons beneath her chin, and they were pinned there with a glistening moonstone. Shamelessly he moved his chair, that he might see her face. It was turned reverently to the bishop; all its delicate lines were subdued into a gracious harmony of expectant feeling. There was a grave, mystic rapture in her eyes that smote Kittredge with a sense of awe. She must believe herself in the house of the Lord; he had been tarrying all the time in the Chapel of St. Anastasia. He looked away from her to the preacher and listened for a few sentences, then he glanced back at her with a sort of wonder; yet to have had her gaze at him as she did at the bishop. Salem would have been quite willing to preach the sermon.

When the service was over he waited for her in the porch, just as he had seen the swains do in his native town of Burridge, and they strolled back to the Occidental, down the narrow plank-walks, side by side. He felt more at ease in his old black Sunday suit than in white flannel. He felt that it even gave his conversation a certain weight. Not that their

talk was peculiarly profound : it turned first
upon Mrs. Atterbury, who had preferred to attend the Unitarian service, as was her wont;
then back upon the growth of ritualism, until
both remembered they had already argued
the question the evening before; and finally
upon Frederic Pitman. She asked, innocently
enough, where Mr. Pitman was, and when
Salem remarked inadvertently that he had not
yet risen, her face clouded, as if a hint had
been given of some irregularity of life. She
even went so far as to admit that there had
been rumors at Magnolia that he was not entirely " nice." Salem tried to explain, found
it a trifle embarrassing, and then, his honest
soul filled with sympathy for the boy's effort to
reform, he frankly told her the facts concerning Pitman's peculiar malady. She listened,
at first uncomfortably, then eagerly, at last
with something of that passion for reforming
things and people without which a good American woman is incomplete.

" So you see how it is, Miss Atterbury,"
he concluded. " He isn't a bad fellow. A
kinder, more thoughtful man doesn't exist;
and he has ability, too. As he told me," and
Salem's voice trembled as he quoted words
that had made a deep impression upon himself,

" ' if man, woman, or dog would stick by me, I could beat it.' "

She looked up at him, with a quick glance of sympathy. He had never seen her eyes so lovely. "May I tell my aunt?" she asked. They were just passing between the stone gate-posts of the Occidental grounds. "She will be so glad to hear this. She knows Mr. Pitman's mother—the sweetest little woman, she says. And perhaps, if we could make it pleasanter for Mr. Pitman, we might help you now and then. It is a very noble thing you are doing, may I say so? It is quite worth devoting one's whole summer to, Mr. Kittredge."

He had said nothing about that trip around the world.

VII

A T dinner that afternoon the head-waiter assigned to Kittredge and Pitman seats at one of the side tables, at the very one, indeed, where the Atterbury ladies already had places. Pitman considered this advancement as the slowly ripening fruit of the fee he had given on arrival, but Salem inferred, and rightly, that Mrs. Atterbury had consented to join the informal league for the moral amelioration of the Inebriate, and had taken this initial step. Young Pitman's deportment was certainly such as to repay all efforts taken in his behalf. His manners were irreproachable ; indeed, Miss Rachel could not fail to notice that he understood some trifling technicalities better than Mr. Kittredge. No professional diner-out had a richer fund of anecdote, or a more charming fluency. Salem was immensely proud of him, and throughout dinner endeavored with entire success to keep himself in the background.

Mrs. Atterbury in particular was delighted

with Frederic Pitman. She had reached that age when she wanted to have bright talkers around her, especially if they were good-natured young men with a turn for practical affairs. She liked to see a young fellow efficient; she enjoyed knowing that Pitman had been so successful in pushing the Primitive Pellets; she even gave a decided Pellet contour to the conversation, to Miss Rachel's dismay. Mrs. Atterbury had absolutely none of the romanticism that threw a vague but delightful haze over some of her niece's projects. What she saw at all, she saw very clearly, and she flattered herself that in every-day matters she usually knew the end from the beginning. In her way, too, she was democratic. If the Pitmans could do with Pellets what the Atterburys, from the old Colonel down, had done with Leather, why should they not? And, finally, she was quite sure that if young Pitman had discovered the specific for fever and ague, he would be bright enough to know whether her architect had made a mistake in that winding staircase.

Dinner over, she announced an intention of inspecting the cottage, and invited the young men to accompany her. "The cottage again —and Sunday, too, Auntie!" exclaimed Miss Rachel—but she went for her bonnet. The

new summer home of the Atterburys was down
behind the Occidental, on the thick-wooded
rocky shore.   The timbers were already raised,
and the ground-plan of the rooms could easily be
traced.   Salem and Miss Atterbury picked their
way over the unfloored joists for awhile, but she
declined to mount the ladder to the second
story, and the result was that they soon took
shelter upon the shady side of the structure,
where they sat upon a couple of lime barrels
and talked about the " Golden Legend."   Mrs.
Atterbury and the Inebriate were meantime
settling the stair problem from an advantageous
position upon the second floor.   It all proved
very informal and agreeable, and Salem was
thoroughly confident, as the four sauntered home
together toward sundown, that such companionship would do a great deal for young Pitman—
indeed for anybody.   As for himself, this whole
day, after such a night, had been Paradise following the Inferno.   He could almost fancy
that he saw, anywhere in the swiftly changing
tints of that northern sunset, the mystic rose.

In the course of the next week or two the
young men fell into the habit of strolling down
to the Atterbury cottage of an afternoon, and
chatting with the ladies, who where almost sure
to be there.   The proprietor of the billiard-

room they had patronized supposed they had
taken to playing at the Pelican tables, and was
grieved at heart, but even Pitman enjoyed himself better watching the workmen, and allowing
the ladies to elevate his moral tone, than he did
playing billiards against an opponent like Kittredge. For Salem this period marked an epoch.
It is a distinct stage in a man's social evolution
when he acquires the proper use of the word
" charming," and the theologue, in the stimulating atmosphere of Mount Desert, learned to
prolong the first syllable with a tender enthusiasm that assured his social success.

Occasionally the four took long buckboard
drives together over the perfect roads of the
little island. Mrs. Atterbury usually preferred
the front seat, just behind the driver, where she
could jump easily in case of accident ; and the
Inebriate sat with her, partly because she rather
petted him, and partly, as he said, out of a general disposition to see the wheels go round.
He had that inquisitive temper, that presence of
mind and immediateness of interest which fitted him admirably for the companionship of a
woman who liked to feel herself a part of this
present world—even when driving through the
odorous, lonely woods of Mount Desert ; while
as for the two young people on the back seat, so

far as their joining in the stream of talk was concerned, they might as well have been—where in fact Salem most often was—in the seventh heaven. When the conversation of this pair grew too transcendental, Mrs. Atterbury was wont to insist upon a change of seats, and then young Pitman, more pleased than he would have cared to show, did his best to entertain the niece. He was somewhat afraid of her. He admired her face and the elaborate simplicity of her gowns; she did not bore him with Ibsen and Buddhism and University Extension; and yet he knew very well that she was the sort of girl who "organized" the poor and worked altar-cloths and looked askance upon Inebriates, and he held her therefore in proper awe.

Miss Rachel, if the truth were known, was often quite willing to relinquish the misty uplands where she had been wandering with the theologue for a more commonplace conversational saunter with the heir to the Primitive Pellets. She was amused with the Inebriate, as was everyone else, and in addition to that she was conscious of a sort of maternal pity for him—being a whole two years older. Then, too, she had a chivalric sympathy for the efforts Kittredge was making to save him from his one error. It seemed to her, as she had said, a very noble thing to do, and she felt a glow of ardor at the thought that she also might be an instrument. Miss Atterbury was something of a saint, and had all the potentialities of a martyr. She was full, for instance, of those renunciatory ideas which cause high-bred girls to throw themselves away on half-bred ministers; but one is not always equal to one's highest devotion, and it was with some positive comfort—under a lesser heat, as it were, of the sacrificial flame—that she endeavored to be very nice to Freddie Pitman.

Kittredge, overhearing scraps of her friendly talk with the young fellow, was delighted to see them get on so well together. He had, perhaps, been a little jealous of Pitman, that morning upon the Olivette, but now that he knew Miss Atterbury better, he could afford to smile at the memory. He resigned Freddie to her, as one gives up the reins to a better driver than himself; his responsibility for the Inebriate had been lightened by so much since he had walked home from church with Miss Rachel, and had had intuition enough to tell her frankly about Pitman's malady!

There were but two things that really troubled Kittredge, as those delicious weeks went by. One of them was the Honourable Plantagenet.

This interesting specimen of his order persisted in promenading the Occidental veranda with Miss Atterbury, deep in the discussion of Americanisms — a harmless recreation of which Salem thought him altogether too fond. Once or twice he was asked to join their buckboard parties, and Mrs. Atterbury had consulted him about the quartered oak wainscoting of her dining-room, having a sort of idea that quarterings was a familiar term to the British aristocracy. The day that Kittredge and Pitman rowed the ladies out to inspect the White Squadron, the Honourable Plantagenet was on board the flagship, renewing a Washington acquaintance with a multitude of lovely lieutenants ; and he presented all of them to Miss Atterbury and her aunt, leaving their civilian escorts to examine the new guns at their leisure. Even the imperturbable Pitman growled upon this occasion, and when the burly Englishman, at his own request, steered their boat back to the wharf, Kittredge was quite consoled for his own awkwardness as an oarsman by observing how thoroughly he had succeeded in wetting him down.

One evening, too, when the Sleighton-Crushtons gave a huge reception at their cottage in honor of somebody or other, and Mrs. Atterbury had secured cards for the two young men, Kittredge felt again a sudden suspicion of the attaché. When the dancing began, Salem retreated to a dark little balcony, and grimly watched a more brilliant scene than he had ever witnessed, caring only to see how often Plantagenet was dancing with Miss Atterbury. Once, seeing him advance toward her, and the Inebriate, who was doing his duty like a man, approach from an opposite direction, Salem pushed his way awkwardly across the ball-room and succeeded in keeping himself between the Englishman and Miss Rachel, until Freddie had carried her off; whereupon Salem beat a triumphant retreat to his balcony. She came out there afterward, with her fingers upon Pitman's elbow, and chatted a moment with Kittredge in most delightful intimacy, the light gleaming from her arms and shoulders; but she shivered in the sea-air, and Pitman folded a swan's-down wrap about her, and took her back.

The occupants of No. 37 rarely discussed Mrs. Atterbury's niece, but after their return from the reception that night Salem asked the Inebriate confidentially if he thought that Plantagenet was paying Miss Atterbury "serious attention." Young Pitman answered, with encouraging promptness:

" He looked like paying serious attention to you, Kittie, I can tell you, when you shipped that cold water into his waistcoat the other day ! Serious about the other matter ? " A quizzical smile passed over Freddie's pert, sun-burnt face, and he leaned over to untie his shoestrings. " Doubted ; it's the summer season, my dear, and he has nothing else to do. Besides, he hasn't a sovereign in the world, you know, and not much chance of ever succeeding to any. Mrs. Atterbury would never let her niece be picked off by a man who had nothing but an attaché's salary."

" But does she understand about the Honourable ? "

" Hm—humph ! " asserted Pitman, gathering up his shoes and other articles of his faultless attire, preparatory to retiring to the inner room.

" How do you know ? " persisted Salem.

" I may have told her myself," said the Inebriate, carelessly. " Everybody knows it. Good-night, Kittie." And Salem went to sleep comforted, though he woke up in the middle of the night and tried to calculate the probable difference between an attaché's salary and a minister's.

From his second subject of anxiety, also, he

was relieved by a word of his *protégé*. As the sailing day of the Richard H. Gulick drew near, Salem found himself shrinking from the idea of that trip around the world as from something unthinkable. So much had changed since he had promised J. Howard Pitman to make a trial with the boy! Every Monday there had come a letter from the proprietor of the Primitive Pellets, closing invariably with " God bless you," and Salem had a sore struggle between his sense of responsibility and his new dreams. He could not go around the world; yet perhaps he might stay with young Pitman awhile longer, if he was wanted, and if —Ah! there were so many "ifs," and his heart was all in a tumult.

One evening in the second week of August the two young men strolled over to the Atterbury cottage after dinner, there to await the ladies, who had proposed building a drift-wood fire down by the rocks. The workmen were making rapid progress, in spite of Mrs. Atterbury's frequent changes in the plans, and Salem said something about the attractiveness of the building.

"Of course it is," assented the Inebriate, as they sat down upon a pile of lath. " Mrs. Atterbury ought to have a fine house. She can pay for it, and she deserves it. She's getting too old to knock around from pillar to post every summer; she ought to settle down."

"It's a great thing," said Salem earnestly, though somewhat vaguely.

"Correct you are, Kittie. I'll be hanged if I haven't about made up my mind to settle down myself."

He had a whimsical look that made Salem answer "Yes?" without knowing exactly how to take him.

"Well, why not? I'm sick of the road, though J. Howard doesn't suspect it. He'd like nothing better than to give me a half-interest at the Works, and I don't know but I shall be just filial enough to let him be happy in the way he likes best, eh?"

"And the R. H. Gulick?" ventured Kittredge, his heart beating fast.

Pitman fluently consigned the R. H. Gulick to Halifax.

"Kittie, do you really see us going round the world together on a brig?"

"No," Salem confessed, with an immense relief.

"Nor I either. We couldn't even play billiards." Then the sardonic amusement faded out of his face as he added, seriously: "It isn't necessary, Kittie. You know what I mean. If I'm not on the road, I can—there can be somebody to look out for me, as you did, and stick by me. See?"

His eager confidence in himself was hard to resist. Salem could not help wondering why he had never been willing to try so simple a plan before, and yet the boy's new purpose furnished a ready way out of his own perplexity. "I'll write your father to-morrow and resign," he said, rather awkwardly. "My six weeks are about up."

"It's been a great six weeks for me," said the grateful Inebriate. "I never had anyone stand right by me at the very dot the way you did."

"It's been a great six weeks for me," murmured Salem, but he was not thinking of the aid rendered to young Pitman. A straight path seemed opening before his vision, and a long, long vista down it.

Miss Atterbury appeared over the brow of the hill, followed by her aunt, and the Inebriate rose, threw away his cigar, and joined her, while Salem sat there two or three minutes longer, in a sort of rapture. Then he helped Mrs. Atterbury pick her way through the *débris* behind the cottage, down to a cosey nook among the rocks by the shore — his heart reproaching him somewhat for not having always shown Mrs. Atterbury quite the attention deserved by a person so kind and bright — and motherly.

All four set to work gathering driftwood, but they waited till deep dusk before lighting the pile, and then found that the dead seaweed was too damp to burn. Salem struck match after match in vain. At last Miss Atterbury declared that she had set her heart upon having this fire, and that she was going up to the cottage for some shavings. Pitman politely insisted upon accompanying her. Kittredge remained on his knees, blowing ineffectually at the smoking seaweed, while Mrs. Atterbury, wrapped in a big shawl, was perched not unpicturesquely upon a bowlder.

" Haven't you any paper ? " she asked.

Kittredge felt through his pockets. His new flannel suit had grown unpresentable, and he was wearing that night the ministerial garb in which he had left Boston. " Here seems to be something," he said, pulling a pamphlet from the inside pocket. " Hullo ! " He tore off the cover and touched a match to it ; the impervious face of J. Howard Pitman crinkled and shrivelled into flame.

Salem tore out page after page, and laid them carefully above the first.

" It isn't anything you care for ? " inquired Mrs. Atterbury.

" Hardly ; " he smiled. " Look there ! " The ghastly portraits of Southern sufferers from fever and ague, before and after using the Primitive Pellets, were writhing into distorted and horrible shapes, and the driftwood was catching fire from them. " It's the Pitman catalogue," he explained. " I'm glad Frederic wasn't here "—and he thought of the delicate way in which Miss Rachel had turned Pitman's back upon the advertisement, that morning on the Olivette.

" Really ! " said Mrs. Atterbury, in some amusement. " I should have liked to see it. I am told that the Pellets are a very valuable property."

" I suppose so," rejoined Kittredge, with the indifferent air of a man whose interests are beyond the reach of moth and rust.

" Oh, yes," she continued. " Mr. Pitman told me the other day that a syndicate had offered a certain sum to buy them out. It was very large indeed. He has a lovely mother," she added, rather inconsequentially.

" I dare say," replied Kittredge, absently.

It had dawned upon him that here was the
time and place to speak to Mrs. Atterbury, and
the blood flamed into his temples at the thought.
He did not know how to begin, but he felt
that to take her niece from her without warning would be hardly honest.

" She is something of an invalid," Mrs. Atterbury proceeded, " and I think privately that
she is too strong a churchwoman. Rachel,
now, wouldn't be jarred by that at all. Is
Mr. Pitman an Episcopalian ? "

" Do you mean J. Howard ? " He was
still wondering how to begin.

" No, no. Mr. Frederic."

" He ! Oh—Excuse me, yes—I think so."
Her mind seemed to dwell upon Pitman, and
he thought he might use this fact to lead up to
his own suit.

" Pitman and I were looking at the cottage
to-night before you came," he began. His
voice trembled in spite of him. " It seemed
very pretty—and homelike, you know."

" Yes," she said, enthusiastically, " and I
believe the architect was right about that staircase, after all ! Mr. Pitman said he was, the
moment he saw it."

" Pitman thought it was very homelike," he
repeated. " The house, I mean—not the stair-

case. It really made him think of settling down—and I thought so too. Don't you think a young man needs a—sort of—home?"

"Of course," she responded, cheerfully. "I hope you will preach that doctrine when you get into the pulpit, Mr. Kittredge. And he told you something about settling down?"

"Oh, he mentioned it," said Salem, bent now upon getting her attention away from Pitman; "but I must say I feel much as he does. I want to settle down myself."

There was a long pause, and he threw a couple of old boat-ribs upon the fire before going on. "I feel as if the time had come——" He hesitated, and she broke in cordially:

"Well, I should think you would, Mr. Kittredge, after studying all these years a system of theology that no one really believes, you see. It must be a great pleasure to get at practical work. We think it has been a wonderful thing for Mr. Pitman to have you with him. It has done so much for him!"

"It isn't about Pitman that I wanted to speak," he began once more, impatiently; "it's about——"

"Hullo, Kittie!" called out the Inebriate's gay voice from the top of the cliff. "Stir up your fire, so that we can see the way down.''

Kittredge gave a savage thrust at his bonfire, and the two young people came scurrying down the narrow path into its circle of light.

'' Where are the shavings ? '' inquired Mrs. Atterbury.

'' We saw Mr. Kittredge's fire, and so we didn't bring them down,'' answered Freddie.

Mrs. Atterbury nodded, and moved along upon her bowlder to make room for her niece. But the girl seemed to be shivering : she knelt on the other side of the fire, and drawing off her gloves, held out her slender hands to the blue and green flame of the driftwood, and as she smiled across at Salem through the blazing smoke, he knew he had never seen her so beautiful.

'' It was good of you, Mr. Kittredge,'' she said ; '' you are always doing something for us.''

He made no answer, except to look into her eyes, and he forgot all about her aunt and Freddie Pitman.

They sat a long time around the fire, but no one talked much. It was enough to watch the driftwood burning, and to breathe the pine odors that the land breeze brought down to greet the sea. They waited till the fire had died quite away, and then scrambled up the cliff-path toward home. Kittredge offered his help to Miss Atterbury, and the very instant he felt her light, firm touch upon his arm he knew that he should speak to her on the morrow.

VIII.

WHEN the morrow came fate favored him.
He wrote a letter to J. Howard Pitman,
explaining respectfully that Frederic had plans
which rendered it imperative that the trip
around the world should be given up. The
young man would himself communicate them
shortly; for the present it was enough to say
that Frederic was contemplating a step which
would give his father great pleasure. Salem
added that though it scarcely seemed necessary
that the peculiar relation between Frederic and
himself should continue longer, he nevertheless
felt so grateful that his lot had been cast in Bar
Harbor that summer that he would cheerfully
put himself at the service of the Pitmans at any
time, should the young man again desire a companion, and provided his own circumstances
would. in any way allow him to do so. Kittredge was rather pleased with this note; it
seemed to say enough without saying too much.

He went to the hotel office to mail it and
found there a letter which was singularly oppor-

tune. It was an invitation to preach as a candidate in a desirable church near Boston upon the following Sunday. He had known before that his name had been mentioned there, but had supposed the church and parish would prefer an older man. It was a most cordial letter ; he felt that it meant a call ; and he strode up and down the side veranda of the Occidental with a nervous smile upon his lips. He told himself to keep steady ; he had seen his Andover friends do such fatuous things just because they were sure of an income and knew they could marry someone at once ! Yet here was the call plainly in sight ; it was a strong church, even a rich church ; Mrs. Atterbury would know all about it ; he could give the letter to Mrs. Atterbury, or read it to her himself, and she would perceive that her niece was not to be asked to starve in a country parish. As for Rachel, he believed she understood him already, and that a word would be enough. Women had such a wonderful knack at guessing !

The ladies were out sketching that morning, and Salem paced the veranda a long time. The Honourable Plantagenet took a few turns with him, and Kittredge found the Englishman not so bad a fellow after all ; he was amused that he had ever been jealous of him. Pitman was deep in a novel; he seemed rather ill-tempered—for a wonder—and Kittredge did not disturb him. They had a dull lunch together. Mrs. Atterbury and her niece were lunching at the Sleighton-Crushtons, and afterward went directly to a tennis party. The afternoon seemed interminable. The Inebriate stuck moodily to his novel and his cigar, while Kittredge walked to Spouting Horn and back, to compose his mind—and his speech to Mrs. Atterbury.

At dinner the young men were again alone. Pitman volunteered the information that the ladies were dining at the Cuttyhunk; there were some friends of his mother over there; he supposed he would have to go over there himself. Until dark, Kittredge sat in the office, trying to read the Boston papers. Then he remembered that the Olivette was lying at her wharf for some repairs, having run down a schooner in the fog the night before; and he sauntered down to the boat to inquire if she would be ready to make the return trip the following evening. It occurred to him that this would give him time Saturday to run up to Andover and select one of his written sermons. The purser answered his questions and still he lingered upon the Olivette's immaculate deck. He found the place by the rail where he had

stood that wonderful morning with Miss Atterbury, and he looked over into the black water
lapping against the wharf-piles, and saw again
her hand and arm as she pointed out the nautilus.

Loud talking and laughter at the bow, together with brilliant flashes of light, roused him
from his dream, and he strolled forward. The
quartermaster and second officer were descant-
ing to a few Mount Desert cronies upon the
virtues of their electric search-light; why, at
Port Tampa, the winter before, they had sight-
ed a fish-line clear at the other end of the big
pier; there would be no use trying to run a
blockade nowadays if those duffers on the
White Squadron had search-lights half as good;
and then the quartermaster began to flash the
slender cone of dazzling light hither and thither
on the water and the wharf, out upon the canoes and yachts lying at anchor, up against
the rocky path under the Club House, and
even far over to the huge side of the Occidental, which it illuminated with a pale circle.
Suddenly the quartermaster turned the projector
upon the wharf again; it smote blindingly in
the faces of a sailor and a woman who was
talking confidentially with him. The crowd
laughed, but the woman kept his arm, and
Salem liked her for it.

"Try for them folks on the Cuttyhunk piazza," suggested someone; "it ain't much over a hundred yards."

The quartermaster turned to adjust the screws, and even as he did so, an unaccountable presentiment took possession of Kittredge's mind. He felt horribly certain that he was to see Miss Atterbury with the Honourable Plantagenet at her elbow; the thought seized him that he knew but one side of her, that the world of germans and tennis parties and dinners and cottages was one into which he had scarcely had a glimpse, that she belonged to that world in spite of herself, and that she would marry the Honourable Plantagenet after all! He grasped hard at the capstan to stop his trembling; the voices of the men buzzed in his ears; then the white rays were flashed full upon the Cuttyhunk, and he saw her.

She was standing quite at the end of the veranda, with the swan's-down wrap about her shoulders, and seemed as if she were smiling straight at him. The Honourable Plantagenet was nowhere in view. Of those near her, Salem recognized only the diminutive figure and amiable countenance of the Inebriate, and a tumultuous joy swept over him. He might still claim her; she belonged to no man else!

He walked the Corniche road for an hour, to give her time to get back to the Occidental. He abandoned all idea of speaking first to the aunt; she went utterly out of his mind; he saw only Rachel's slender figure wrapped in swan's-down, and her eyes seemed still smiling into his.

Miss Atterbury had gone to her room, the clerk told him when he came in, and he hurried to No. 37 to get a card to send up to her. She would come down to the drawing-room, he knew; they had sat there together a dozen times; there was a door leading out to the dark side veranda; he could ask her to walk a little with him, and then——

He opened the door of No. 37. A man was sitting on the bed, with face buried in his hands. In a startled moment Salem recognized the Inebriate, and he struck a match and lighted the gas. Pitman looked at him; there were tears in his eyes.

"I guess I'm rather broken up," he said. "Sit down, Kittie; I want to tell you something. I proposed to Miss Atterbury last night, and she has just given me her answer. It takes hold of me pretty hard; I haven't been just the sort of man I might, you see. You know all about it, and of course she does. I told her everything; every blessed thing; a fellow ought to, with that sort of girl. And it's knowing all that—and that she knows it—that—it breaks me all up!"

It was getting too incoherent for the amazed theologue to follow. "You mean," he broke in, a certain righteous hardness mingling with the sympathy in his shaking voice, "that she refused you on account of your record."

"No!" cried Pitman, leaping up, with the queerest smile around his mouth, "that's just what she ought to have done, but she didn't. She accepted me in spite of my record! She believes in me! I'm an engaged man, Kittie; queer, isn't it? Put it there!"

But Kittredge's hands were griping the back of a chair, and his rosy face was gray.

"I can't," he groaned, "I can't. The fact is——"

He stopped. Pitman stared at him an instant, then nodded as if to himself, with a sudden comprehension.

"I didn't suppose *that*," he murmured, slowly. "Of course I knew you liked her. I'm—I'm awfully sorry. It's hard luck, Kittie. Please," and with a boyish timidity the Inebriate put out his hand again.

The Czar's Diamond

THE CZAR'S DIAMOND

IN the heart of Old Berlin, hid away behind the Börse, there stood until very lately a tiny Gothic church. It was so small, and the street upon which it faced was so insignificant, that one might live in Berlin all his life and never hear of it. It was very old, much the oldest church in the city, though no one knew exactly the time when its stout walls and quaint, pointed arches had been raised. Yet this spot, at least, had once been occupied by the chapel of a hospital built for the Crusaders, who brought back from the Holy Land the pestilence and leprosy. Records of the thirteenth century tell of this, and all through the Middle Ages the hospital and its chapel stood there, the latter always bearing the same name, the Church of the Holy Ghost. A hundred years ago three aged lindens were still to be seen in front of it; and the tradition was that these had been planted twigs downward by three falsely accused persons, who proved through the miraculous growth, to the satisfaction of mediæval law, that they were guiltless before God. Here the orphans of the city used to come for worship, after there were no more Crusaders; and in the eighteenth century, when a powder explosion had shattered the great garrison church near by, the soldiers of the father of the great Frederick were marched in here on Sunday mornings to listen to the reformed faith. Some old people now living can remember when a congregation of converted Jews used to gather in the chapel; after the Hebrews came an organization of Reformed Catholics; and thirty years ago there were special services here for *droschke* drivers. The old walls, therefore, have harbored strange assemblies, first and last, though in the latter years there has been hardly any congregation at all. Precisely at noon, each Sunday, the sexton carried out two little standards and placed them on the pavement in front of the chapel, for a sign that wagons must go through a neighboring street and make the spot even quieter; and then a few persons, never more than twenty or thirty, most of them old people who lived near by, came in to the service. There was a little organ in the gallery, and two or three students of theology usually attended in order to help along the feeble singing. But the Lutheran pastor preached with strange earnestness, and it may be that there was just as sincere worship in the chapel as there was in the crowded Dom, not far distant upon the opposite side of the Spree.

Nevertheless, the time came at last for the abandonment of the old building, and the removal of the congregation to a brand - new chapel. One bright March midday the closing service was held, and the good pastor's voice trembled somewhat as he preached from the text : "Except ye turn and become as little children, ye shall not enter into the Kingdom of Heaven." His auditors were more numerous than usual, and among them were an elderly man and a little girl, who for months past could have been seen every Sunday upon a front seat in the queer old gallery. The pastor had inquired once of the sexton who these persons were, but all the sexton could ascertain was that the man's name was Engel, and that the yellow-haired girl was a daughter of Engel's landlady. Herr Engel always watched the preacher with grave attention. He wore usually a skull-cap, he had a square, immobile face, smoothly shaven, his figure was rather short and heavy, and he was forced to climb slowly up and down the gallery stairs, seeming to like to hold the girl's hand as he did so. To see him upon this March day, one would have guessed that the elderly church-goer was a retired artisan or man of some petty business, ending his days in peace, and preparing his soul for the close by listening to the serious words of the thin-faced pastor. The guess would have been partly right. Herr Engel was ending his days, and he came to the Chapel of the Holy Ghost to seek his soul's good; but behind his tranquil face there was a mind tortured by memory, a will wrestling ever, and ever overcome and growing weaker; for the man was not what he seemed to be. He was an Englishman and a thief.

In the spring of 1854 a clever theft of imperial diamonds at St. Petersburg was for a day or two the theme of comment in the European press. The outbreak of war in the Crimea had thrown the Czar's palace into momentary confusion, and the robbery was so skilfully executed that only the merest accident gave the clew by which the thieves were caught. All the jewels were recovered except one, a stone of high value. The criminals were promptly dealt with, and though the police never found what was done with the missing diamond, yet what mattered a single stone, worth six thou-

sand rubles though it were, in that battle summer? When those members of the small
English colony who wished to leave the city
were allowed to do so, no one thought of
searching Richard Angell, an ingenious locksmith of thirty, who had gained high wages in
Russia, but whose highest wage of all was the
diamond conveyed to him for his secret share
in the robbery at the palace. He brought this
diamond with him to Berlin, he had kept it for
more than thirty years, and it gleamed now
with an evil light in his memory, as he sat in
the Chapel of the Holy Ghost and sought in
vain to find his peace with God.

To think that one thing will spoil a man's
life! All he had done was to make some duplicate keys. The other thieves had been honest
with him and had given him what they promised:
this one stone. At first, after coming to Berlin
and securing work at his trade, he did not dare
to sell the jewel, for the risk would have been
too great. He used, nevertheless, to speculate
about the price and to plan what he would
do with the money. The diamond ought to
be precious, he thought to himself, with a kind
of humor, for he had bought it with his honesty.
Little by little he shrank from the idea of selling it, at least for the present. Often he took

it at night from its hiding-place, and for hours
watched how the candle-flame was flashed back
from its facets, how the stone grew luminous
within, shining now white and cold like snow,
then warm as Crimean sunlight. This Russian
diamond seemed a live thing, and fascinated
him. The months went by and then the years,
before he knew it; the diamond became a part
of his life, and he grew to love it as other men
love women. He used to laugh at himself
sometimes, and wonder what would come of it
all. It was absurd enough: a young fellow,
all alone in the world, with no one dependent
upon him—he might travel and see Europe, he
might do so many things with the price of that
stone—and yet here he filed away in the German workshop, amused himself at night by
looking at his big diamond, and did not even
care to see England again! But so he went on
years and years. The steady, silent workman
felt a gulf opening between himself and other
men; he had something that was all his own.
The Angells were a lonely folk, his grandmother
had once told him, and did not need other people so much as most. It did not occur to him
particularly that he wanted friends. He was on
good terms enough with his fellow-workmen, to
be sure, and every Thursday night for a long

time had his regular seat at a *Stammtisch* with them, in a quiet little place in the Spandauer Strasse. But he never added much to the joviality of the company, and when, shortly after the Franco-Prussian War, the new Rathhaus was completed, and the other locksmiths decided to set up their *Stammtisch* in the huge, crowded Rathskeller, Engel slipped out of the circle, almost without their knowing he was gone. Occasionally he took a stroll with an acquaintance in the Thiergarten on a Sunday afternoon, but more commonly he went alone, sometimes walking as far as Charlottenburg, where he would hunt out a corner in some garden, under the horse-chestnut trees, and have a glass of Moabit beer with a bit of bread and cheese, before tramping back to his lodgings. He used to watch the Sunday crowds with some curiosity, but with no great interest. All those men and women had their own affairs ; they did not care for him. Well, he did not care for them ; he had his own affairs, too.

Gradually he came to wonder how he could ever have thought of selling the diamond. As well sell himself; nay, the stone was himself: had he not sold himself to gain it ? There was a dreary sort of amusement in this thought of the identity of himself with the stone, when the idea first occurred to him, and it amused him twenty years. He smiled at it sometimes while working at his bench, and murmured something in English; then the other workmen would eye him and whisper among themselves. As he grew older he stooped more, got heavier in figure, and walked less on Sundays. He had always been a diligent hand at his trade, but at last he took so few holidays, and hammered away so taciturnly, that even those who had been on friendly terms with him were inclined to grow provoked at his lack of sociability, and to discover that he was queer. Richard Engel only dropped his head lower over his work and talked less than ever. But one day he felt a terrible pain at his heart, and went to see a doctor. The doctor examined him carefully.

"You are a locksmith, you say? You have been bending over your table too much. You should stop work, or if you will go on, it must be at your risk. Have you anything laid up, Herr Engel?" It was the most natural question in the world, but the patient's face paled with terror. If he had anything laid up! "No," he stammered, "not much."

For months he remained idle, and then for the first time his conscience gave him real uneasiness. He was not so very old; he had never thought much of how the matter might end ; of course it was a sin, this queer adventure with a diamond, yet the thing seemed more strange than sinful. But that sudden pain in his chest woke him. Death, then, was waiting at the end of his experiment. He found that he had been playing a cunning secret game, with his soul for stake, and had all these years been losing. The months that he was out of the shop were a torture to him ; he grew restless, nervous, imaginative. He thought of restitution, but when he drew the brilliant from its case to look at it, he learned how he had grown to love this stone that had mastered his life. He could not give it up. It was possible to sell it now, and to live the rest of his days upon the money, without risking again the terrible pain in his chest that came from the locksmith work, but he could not bring himself to the thought of parting with it. Sell that diamond ? No ! Nevertheless his conscience stung him so in these idle days of brooding that he went back to his old place. Here he found employment for his hands, but the sharp twitches in his chest kept warning him and turned his thoughts to death ; death led him to the fear of judgment ; this brought him back to the diamond, and the diamond to his spoiled life, and his life to the inevitable death ; such was the inexorable circle in which Herr Engel's mind travelled, and his will had become too weak to break the circuit, and still one year after another slipped by.

It was of all this that he was thinking, on that sunny March noon, in the gallery of the chapel, while gazing vacantly at the pastor. Is it a good deal? A drowning man will think of all that in a single moment's time, and Herr Engel felt like a drowning man. It was the last service in the old chapel, and he felt that he would not attend one in the new. He had come here at first with Gretel, the ten-year-old daughter of his landlady, and had taken a fancy to the Chapel of the Holy Ghost. It reminded him of a country church in Kent where he had always gone in boyhood, and he fell into the habit of coming regularly, hoping, in a puzzled and indefinite sort of way, to find here some reconciliation. But he had found nothing ; he was a thief, and he knew it ; he could not part with the diamond, and he knew it ; he dared not die and face God without making some reparation for his sin, and yet he could not even make up his mind to confess. Though he tried to listen now, he heard but little of the pastor's last sermon, and the little that he heard he could not understand. It was about children and the Kingdom of Heaven.

When the discourse was finished, and the clergyman had dismissed his people in peace, Engel felt as if the waters were closing above his head ; but the blue eyes of the child with him seemed even happier than usual. She jumped upon the seat and helped him on with his overcoat, and then kept tight hold of his hand as they came down the narrow stairs. His heart had fluttered hard as he climbed up them, and he crept down slowly, fearfully. He found himself wondering as never before about the life of a child ; it seemed such a strange thing. There was to him something pathetic about this German maiden's holding his hand ; something incomprehensible in the fact that they two should be coming out of the chapel together. They stopped in the porch and Gretel spelled out once more the inscription upon a tablet that commemorated the repair of the chapel in 1597. Then they dropped some pfennigs into the battered tin box for the poor.

" We ought to give a great deal to-day, Herr Engel."

" Yes, Gretel," he answered, " for it is the last time."

"But next week we shall go to the new
chapel; won't we? And perhaps there will be
a new box."

"Perhaps," said Engel.

They turned down a narrow street and came
out upon the bank of the Spree, along which
lay their route homeward to the old house on
the Mühlendamm. It was not a long distance,
but they usually walked slowly, and Gretel
found so much to amuse her on the way, and so
many questions to ask, that the walk seemed
quite an adventure in itself. There were never
such gay throngs of people on this side of the
Spree as on the other, where the museums and
the palace were, and yet Engel and the child
were always sure of seeing some smartly attired
young lieutenant stalking stiffly along the pavement, or a merry *droschke* load of corps-students
in colored caps, or perhaps a stray peasant from
the Spreewald, in his Sunday best. The child
noticed everything: sometimes she would make
Engel stop by the landing over the river to see
the fishermen empty the living freight of their
black boats into the great water-tubs sent from
the fish-market to receive them; and she would
clap her hands when a reluctant eel wound himself skilfully into the meshes of the landing-net
and refused to be shaken into the tub as if he

had a premonition of his fate. But even when there was nothing to see upon the street, Gretel was still satisfied, for then she made Engel tell her stories. He told her all the fairy stories he ever had heard in his boyhood, though many of them she knew as well as he, only that in Grimm they were changed a little. When he could remember no more, he began inventing, and this habit had grown upon him in the months immediately preceding that March day, until he found a certain pleasure in it. The girl always stood ready to help him if his wits gave out, and indeed they called it sometimes just making up stories together. But to-day, as they walked along, his mind was fixed elsewhere than upon her amusement.

"Tell me, Gretel," he said, absently, "could you understand the sermon?"

"Oh, yes! It was beautiful, but just once I was a bad girl; I did not listen. I was thinking of something else."

"You were?" he remarked.

"Yes, and you must guess what it was, and then I will tell you."

"But I am stupid, Gretel."

"Oh, then I will help you. It is small, and yellow. Can't you guess? And lives in a cage—of course you can guess now."

"It is the canary bird you are going to have."

"Right! right!" she cried, gleefully. "You are not stupid at all, Herr Engel. But I would have told you, even if you hadn't guessed;" and Gretel added demurely, "So I was thinking of my canary bird, and forgot about part of the sermon."

"That was not nice," he ventured.

"Oh, there will be so many sermons more," she said, gayly. "But did not you understand it, Herr Engel?"

"No," answered Engel, bluntly. What was the harm in telling the truth to the child?

"Were you thinking of something, too?" she asked.

He was silent.

"Oh, you were, you were, Herr Engel. I will guess, and you must tell me, just as I did you."

"No! no!" he said, sharply, and his heart beat fast and gave him an exquisite pain. "I will tell you something else—I will tell you a story."

It was the readiest escape that occurred to him. She saw that his breath was hurried, and remembered that her mother had told her that Herr Engel must not walk rapidly.

"Let us stop a minute," she suggested, with a quaint air of motherliness, "we have been going so fast, Herr Engel."

They leaned on the iron railing which runs along the stone embankment of the Spree and looked down at the water. Several people were already at the railing near them, watching some of the white sea-birds that find their way up the Spree at the end of every winter, and that were fluttering in the March sunlight from one perch to another, now resting on a pole stuck in the river's bed, now on the fishermen's boats drawn up above the Friedrich bridge, now floating on the water itself—wild, free things, oddly out of place in the centre of the great city. Gretel was enchanted with them, and it was only after some minutes that she asked for the story.

"The story? Oh, yes, let me think," he replied.

He searched his brain, but there was only one story there, and that was his own. The girl had just confessed her little secret to him. They stood together by the water, she still holding his hand. He felt as he had never done before that he was on a level with some-one. He was conscious of a sudden curiosity to know what the child would think of his

secret. It had always seemed to him an un-
natural thing to confess a crime to a friend,
perhaps because he had had no friend to whom
he could unbosom himself, and he had known,
too, that to confess would be to lose the
diamond; but now this curiosity gained hold
upon him. A child was such a strange thing,
and his life was such a strange thing; perhaps
a child would understand it as well as he. But
of course he would not really tell about himself; he would tell only a story; and this appeared to form itself without his will.

"Yes, Gretel, it is a story about—about one
of those white sea-birds."

"Good! I have never heard that," she cried.

"No," he answered.

"Is it long?" she asked. "Because if it
is, you can tell it after dinner."

"Yes, it is long," replied Engel. He
wanted to say: "thirty years long." "No,"
he added quickly, "not so very long either."
She looked puzzled.

"One of those white sea-birds," he went
on,—"no, that is not the way to begin.
There was once a little girl, who saw one of
those birds, and thought she would like to have
it for her own. So she caught it."

"How?" asked Gretel.

" That—that is not in the story. But she caught it, and to keep it from flying away she tied it to her with a string, so that the bird flew over her head wherever she went. It was such a beautiful bird ; only it was not good, and it used to peck at the little girl's fingers and eyes, and so made her trouble always after a while, oh, so much trouble ! ''

" Why didn't she let it go again ? ''

" Because she couldn't untie the string.''

" That was funny,'' said Gretel. " But go on, Herr Engel ; what did she do then ? ''

" She didn't do anything. What could she do ? I said she couldn't untie the string. What could you do, Gretel, supposing it were you, or I ; yes, suppose now it were I ? ''

The child laughed ; it was an odd story. Then she had an idea, and cried triumphantly, " You could cut the string ! ''

" But I can't cut it ! '' he exclaimed, with inward agony.

" Why not ? '' she asked, disappointedly, her mind too full of the problem to notice anything peculiar in the wistful cunning with which he had substituted himself as the actor in the narrative.

" But I can't ! I can't—nor you—suppose it were you—or the little girl.''

Once more Gretel's blue eyes sparkled. "No, suppose it were you, Herr Engel. Do you know what we would do? I would take my scissors and cut it for you, so! snip!"

He looked down at his companion in wonder. Would she really? He forgot her ignorance and innocence, and that he was a man and she a child.

"But what became of the girl in the story?" she questioned.

"I don't know—yet," he replied. "Come, Gretel."

They went on again down the sunny street, which was filled with people enjoying a Sunday holiday. Rather a pleasant-looking pair of companions were these; the elderly, grave man, neatly dressed, stepping carefully, and by his side the decorous German maiden, in her pink hood, cheap cloak, and heavy shoes, with her long braid of yellow hair down her back, and the Lutheran hymn-book in her red-mittened hand. More than one person smiled benevolently at them, as they passed.

"But didn't anyone ever tell you the end of the story?" Gretel protested.

Engel did not hear her. "Suppose," he said, slowly, "it were a stone."

"Suppose what were a stone?"

"In the story," he answered. "Suppose it were not a bird at all, but just a stone. What could we do then—supposing it were I, and you? Tell me, Gretel, what could we do?"

She looked up in his face, a little frightened by the tone of his voice. "You are so funny to-day, Herr Engel." Yet he held her hand so closely that she was reassured, and she repeated, meditatively: "Suppose it were a stone —and it were you—and I; what could we do? Oh, we could do something, you and I, Herr Engel! Let us see." And she nodded wisely, amused at the novel idea.

But they had reached home : one of the huge old houses over the Spree, upon the Mühlendamm. There had once been a long line of them here, but almost all were now demolished. They went under a black archway, across a stone-paved, dismal court, where the snow was fast melting. The locksmith glanced up at the north wall, where hung an ancient wooden sun-dial, under which was painted an hour-glass surmounting a skull, and the legend " *Mors certa sed hora incerta.*" It was nearly two o'clock. Herr Engel's chest hurt cruelly as he climbed the stairs, but he scarcely noticed it; he was intent upon a last vague chance, and he had put that chance into the hands of a child. They stood an instant in the dark entry.

"Put your hymn-book and cloak away," he said, "and then come into my room."

He wished to have a moment's time, and shut the door of his room behind him. Then he took from its secret place the leathern case which he had made long before to cover the diamond, and laid it on the table by the window. Not two minutes had passed since the girl's hand left his, and he felt already the old irresolution. He hesitated for a terrible second; then Gretel knocked at the door and came in, and he knew that he had put his affair—partly at least—out of his own hands, and he felt childishly weak and irresponsible. He was trembling so that he had to sink into his great chair by the table. The room seemed stiflingly hot, and he breathed with difficulty.

"Open the window; it is so close, Gretel," he murmured.

She obeyed, although to her the room seemed cool enough. The spring sunlight was streaming in at the window and resting upon the table where lay the leathern case. Gretel eyed the latter curiously for an instant, and then pulled her chair near Engel's.

"And now shall we finish our story, Herr

Engel? Let's make it up together. What kind of a stone must it be?"

"It belongs to someone else," was his broken answer, "and it has cursed my life, but I cannot give it up. You see, Gretel," he added, drearily, "I can't cut the string."

She could not understand him, and his words perplexed and alarmed her.

"Don't you want to see it, Gretel? Open the case." It did not seem to him that he could stir.

She did as he ordered, and unfastening the case with her slender fingers, saw the glistening stone; she had seen hundreds of them in the windows on the Friedrich Strasse, some that were shinier than this, if not so large; and her courage came back to her. Engel sat gazing steadily at the diamond. It appeared to him duller than it should be, with sunlight on it.

"Whose is it?" the girl asked, in a subdued voice.

"He is dead," Engel replied. "It was a long time ago—and his son is dead, too."

She comprehended more clearly than before that a wrong had been done.

"But the family?" she whispered. "Are they very poor—as poor as we are?" She was ignorant of the value of the stone, but she knew that such things cost a good deal, as much as a dress, perhaps, or a great many baskets of coal.

"The family," said Engel, bitterly, "are richer than the Kaiser." She was silent. Richer than the Kaiser? They must be the fairies. Then she asked, with a child's persistency:

"Why do you want to keep it, if it does you harm?"

"Because I can't cut the string," he groaned. "You have forgotten the story. What can we do, Gretel?" He stared at her with imploring eyes.

She began to be terrified again. She could not grasp his meaning altogether, yet she was sure of this: Herr Engel hated the stone, but he was not able to get rid of it. It must be a bad stone, and as she looked at it, she found herself afraid. Yet the whole adventure seemed to her a kind of fairy story in which she had a part, and that gave her a daring which otherwise she never could have had. With a sudden impulse she took the smooth, cold thing in her fingers. Engel did not move.

"See, Herr Engel," she cried, "let us throw it in the river!" and she tossed it out of the window, and leaping to her feet saw it go flashing down into the muddy water.

With heart beating fast at her own boldness, she turned to Richard Angell. He was sobbing, his face covered with his hands. There was a long silence. Then he rose to his feet, and she saw his happy tears.

"How bright the sun is, Gretel!" he exclaimed. "The summer must be coming, and this summer—this summer——"

But he pressed his hand to his left side; his face flushed swiftly and then turned white, and Gretel was frightened and ran to call her mother.

By the Ill

BY THE ILL

I HAVE never been in love with a woman; at least, not enough in love to ask any woman to marry me. I do not know what that is like, nor do I fancy that any people know except those who have themselves experienced it. Love is like war, they say, and you cannot possibly know anything about real war until you actually smell the powder. It is all a fiction until that acrid odor is in your nostrils, and the singing of the bullets is in your ears. When I was a boy, in North Carolina, I remember running to the pine woods one day with my mother and older brother, and hearing something about General Sherman, and seeing our barns a-blazing up merrily, but though my poor mother said, "Randolph, you will always know now what war is," and the sentence somehow stuck in my memory, I did not, as a matter of fact, know what war was at all. Nor do I know to-day any better, never having heard the bullets nor smelt the powder. No, war and love are not to be talked about by civilians and outsiders. Yet once upon a time it seemed to me that I knew what they both were like, civilian and outsider though I may have been.

It was in Alsace-Lorraine, one June, ten years ago. Many a dragging month I had been "oxing" Sanscrit and Greek for my doctor's degree at Strasburg, and when the thesis had been accepted and the official invitation to the final examination and disputation of "Randolph Merivale, from America," had been duly posted upon the university bulletin board, the old trouble with my eyes came back and I was forced to quit work altogether. For a few days I kept to my lodging in the Hennengasse, to avoid the bright light of the streets, but it grew insufferably hot and malodorous in that ancient alley-way, and so one day I packed my tramping knapsack, put on a big pair of goggles, and marching out of Strasburg by the Ruprechtsauer Allée, struck off through the country toward Fuchs am Buckel.

One can never get to Fuchs am Buckel twice by the same way, so perhaps it is useless to say how one gets there at all. You follow the road easily enough through the village of Ruprechtsau, between the high walls of plastered brick which enclose fruit gardens and vegetable plots, and here and there the grounds of some old manor house, with weather-stained and broken-nosed goddesses still gleaming in the tangled shrubbery. But beyond the straggling village the white hard roads curve and intersect so curiously that I should have despaired of following them, even had the glare not been painful to my eyes. So, knowing the general direction, and that any one of a half-dozen footpaths would serve my turn, I struck into the first that offered itself, and for an hour and a half traversed leisurely the rank fields of grain, the back yards of thrifty Alsatian vegetable-growers, and then along under endless lines of poplars, until a sudden turn brought me out upon the high-road again, and across the wide meadows I caught sight of the heavy clump of woodland against which were the big sloping roofs of Fuchs am Buckel. In spite of the goggles the light was so brilliant that when I reached the familiar goal of student excursions, I could scarcely read the C. FUCHS, RES-TAURATION, painted on the sign. The proprietor of the place remembered me, was able to give me one of the few rooms he kept at the disposal of an occasional lodger, and having darkened the windows and rested a couple of hours, the inflammation in my eyes seemed somewhat relieved, and I was able toward sunset to get down to the garden.

By my favorite table, at the extreme end of the garden, where the black Ill swept close under the big willow that shaded my usual seat, there was a woman. She was seated with her back to me, looking up the river toward the west, as I had sat a dozen times before starting back to Strasburg in the cool of the evening. There was a broad glare upon the glassy water, and perhaps that was why I did not notice her until I was just upon her. That end table had never been a favorite one among the noisy patrons of the *Restauration*, and I had rarely found it occupied before. I remember feeling somewhat disappointed as I took a chair at the next table and rapped for the waitress. While she was getting me some black bread and Münster cheese, a cutlet and a glass of thin white Alsatian wine, the blaze died off from the water, and I pulled my chair around so that I, too, faced the west. The woman at the last table had apparently finished her supper, for a slender jug of seltzer water stood there, surrounded by some plates, from one of which she was gathering bread-crumbs to toss to the ducks in the river. She scarcely turned her head as she snapped the tiny morsels into the current, and

I remember that I did not see her face. She had a short figure, with finely modelled shoulders, and as she swept the last crumbs from her plate over to the struggling, quacking creatures in the river, I noticed that her black dress fitted her extremely well, and that there was a plain ring upon her finger. When the waitress brought my supper the lady had her table cleared, but she paid nothing. She sat there still, and no one came to join her. I finished my own meal, stretched my legs out, American fashion, on an empty chair in front of me, lighted a wretched cigar, and watched the opal tints in the west lose their fire and turn gray. It was nearly dusk, and everyone but ourselves must have left the garden, when old Fuchs made the circuit of the empty tables, gathering up here and there a beer-mug that had been overlooked. He gave me, as usual, a professional " *Guten Abend, Herr Doctor,*" then stopped a moment at the table in front of me, and looking down at the black-dressed woman, said cheerily : " *Eh, comment ça va ? Geht's guet ?* " " *Ganz guet,*" she answered, in a deep full voice, with a marked Alsatian accent. " *Mais comme c'est charmant ici !*" she added. Then, in a still lower tone, she repeated, " *Charmant comme toujours.*"

" *Tu as raison*," said Fuchs, with a satisfied shrug, and passed on.

The evening darkened slowly, and still she did not move. Her head and shoulders were sharply cut against the last pulsation of color on the horizon. A fog began to creep over the surface of the Ill. I was at the end of the second cigar. Suddenly she rose and started toward the house ; in passing my table she stumbled against the chair that upheld my awkwardly extended feet. " *Pardon, monsieur*," she murmured, and before I could touch my hat and mutter an apology she had disappeared.

The next morning, when I came down for my coffee to the main room of the *Restauration*, old Fuchs presented me to her as his niece, Mademoiselle Aubépine. Finding that I was an American student, she addressed me frankly enough in German, though hesitating now and then for a word, and betraying the Alsatian accent I had noticed the evening before. On my asking her whether she knew Strasburg well, she replied simply that she was born in the Blauwolkengasse, which certainly, as I ventured to remark, ought to have given her an unmistakable Strasburg birthright. Thereupon Fuchs interrupted us with a long-winded disquisition upon her relationship to an Alsatian politician who, during the preceding winter, had exhibited himself as a peculiarly ardent member of the Opposition in the Reichstag. While he was talking, I looked at her. She was a woman of thirty, apparently, and thinking of her now, after ten years, I do not remember anything about her that was really beautiful, except her perfectly developed figure and the depth and purity of her voice. Her hazel eyes seemed old, and her hands were old; she talked with the directness and unguardedness of a married woman, looked me straight in the face, gave me the right word when I groped for it—and I liked her.

That afternoon I liked her still better. The imprudence of the day before affected my eyes seriously, and I was obliged to keep indoors. Mademoiselle Aubépine, after a whispered dialogue with Fuchs, came up to me as I was sitting disconsolately in a dark corner of the inn, and asked me if I cared to hear some singing. Now the Merivales were never musical, but I should have been stupider than I seemed had I not eagerly assented. We went into a sort of private sitting-room in the rear of the high seat where Madame Fuchs presided over the affairs of the *Restauration,* and where she could still have us under her eye if she wished. For an hour Mademoiselle Aubépine sang ; French chansons mostly, with a couple of Italian operatic airs, and particularly some Polish slumber songs, to French words ; strange melodies which I did not understand, but which better than all the rest suited her contralto voice, with its somnolent crooning quality. I remember asking her if she did not sing any German songs, and she gave the slightest expression to her shoulders—she was seated at the old piano with her back turned to me—and said, to my wonderment, that she did not. Soon after she stopped singing. She would listen to none of my awkward thanks, saying simply that singing was her business. I was puzzled by this, until old Fuchs informed me confidentially, that evening, that his niece was a *grande artiste* and could go upon the stage if she wished. As it was, she was only a singing-teacher in Nancy, but pupils came to her from Lunéville, and even from Metz, and once there had been talk of her singing in oratorio at Paris !

Yes, I liked Mademoiselle Aubépine. I have never been in love with a woman, as I think I said at the beginning, and it is not my own love-story that I have started to tell. Perhaps it will not even be called a love-story at all, but yet it was about love and war.

I had been at Fuchs am Buckel ten days, and was to leave on the morrow. For the fact that the time had been endurable, I was indebted to Mademoiselle Aubépine. It was she who, in the long forenoons, under the great horse-chestnut trees that shaded the central part of the garden, had read Lamartine and Chateaubriand to me ; these works had been recommended by Madame Fuchs, and indeed they are not so bad. We always talked French after that first morning, and she insisted upon calling me Monsieur Merveille, that being as near to Merivale as she declared she could ever hope to come. Her English was rudimentary, without doubt. For days I tried to teach her one English line—a line that always murmured itself gently to me as we sat at the end of the garden under the willow and watched the Ill move straight toward us and then past, scarcely bending the rushes, so even was its flow—

" Where yon broad water sweetly, slowly glides."

At last she could say it all except " glides," and though she could never pronounce that, her attempt resulted in a word of her own, which was to me as musical. Once or twice, accompanied by Madame Fuchs, we walked in the deep woods, beyond the stone bridge under which half of the Ill shot on its sudden plunge for the Rhine, and she sang each time in the woodland such songs as I have never heard since. But I never knew why she was a singing-teacher, and why she wore a black dress and a ring, until the night before I left.

We had had a sort of family supper together, and out of deference to my choice we were at the end table of the garden. There were four of us: Monsieur and Madame Fuchs, Mademoiselle Aubépine, and I. We had had a vivacious time, and Fuchs had insisted upon opening a bottle of Burgundy in honor of my departure on the morrow. He toasted "America," and I ventured, in response, upon a toast I had never dared propose to an Alsatian: "Alsace-Lorraine." This was in 1880, but all three glanced furtively around before they raised the full glasses to their lips and drained the Burgundy to the last drop. No one spoke; I suspected that I had been indiscreet, and was glad when one of the waitresses called Fuchs away on some matter of business, which in a moment required also the presence of his wife. Mademoiselle Aubépine and I were left alone at the table where she had been sitting on the night I came to Fuchs am Buckel. The sun now, as then, gleamed down the broad polished surface of the Ill and was full in my face. She sat at my left, and I, with eyes still too weak to look up the river, stared down at the table, or, more accurately, at the blue veins of her hand as she toyed with the empty wine-glass, and at the ring upon her finger. I pitied her, vaguely, and wished I had not toasted Alsace-Lorraine, and wished, too—a little—that I was not going away the next morning. And I said something of this, clumsily enough, for she flushed, and doubtless thought I meant something other, or something more, than I did. At any rate she stopped me with a " *Pardon, Monsieur,*" which were the first words she had ever addressed to me.

" Pardon me, Monsieur Merveille, but you do not understand. It is very possible that you will not understand ; yet I shall tell you because you are an American and a *bon camarade.* But one should not speak of Alsace-Lorraine any more. She is dead. ' *Deutsche, Deutsche sind wir alle.*' " She hummed bitterly the opening line of a German patriotic song.

" Yes," said I, with a foolish effort at sympathetic philosophy, " I suppose you must accept facts as they are."

" Accept ? " she cried, in her rapid, impassioned French. " Of course. That is the

worst of it, that one must accept. Those are
fools at Nancy—at Paris—who talk of the *re-
vanche*. We know better, here at Strasburg.
What is done, is done. Look at those walls!''
she exclaimed, with an unsuccessful effort to re-
strain her growing excitement. Her hazel eyes
were changing color, and following their gaze
across the sedge-bordered meadows beyond the
Ill, past a clump of woods and a line of solemn
poplars, I saw the long low parapet of Fort
Fransecky.

" Do you know why that fort is impregna-
ble?'' she demanded. " It is because its walls
are laid in blood."

I felt more awkward than ever, and not
knowing anything to say, snapped some pieces
of biscuit over to the ducks in the Ill. What
was there for me to say?

" Listen, Monsieur Merveille,'' she went on.
" You have no right to speak to me as you did.
I did not know but Madame Fuchs had told
you; I thought you knew why I let myself
treat you *en camarade.*''

" But I knew nothing," I answered, hastily ;
" though I had supposed ''—I hesitated, my
eyes fixed again upon her ring.

" That I had been *fiancée ?* It is true. And
he is dead. It is very true. But how? Listen

to me. You are going in the morning; I
shall not see you again. I have thought of
speaking to you more than once, because I began to fear you were still too young to understand *camaraderie*. You are twenty-five, Monsieur Merveille?"

I nodded. There was a fierce lightness in
her tone, and I dared not interrupt her.

"Well, I am thirty, old enough to say to you
what I please. Only, I wish I had told you before—before to-night."

The brightness had disappeared from the
water now, and I looked up at her steadily.
There were contracted lines upon the low
forehead, a stern set expression about the
mouth, though the round lips were trembling.
I had never seen Mademoiselle Aubépine look
at once so old and so young. Her eyes flashed
in the growing twilight like the eyes of a
girl.

"I was only twenty that August of 1870, and
I had been a *fiancée* six months. He lived in
Kehl, just across the river from Strasburg, you
know, but in Baden. I met him here, at Fuchs
am Buckel. He was second lieutenant in a Baden regiment, but he would have been free that
autumn. He never loved the Prussians—you
know how it was in Baden—but he went with

the rest, like a soldier. I saw him in July, not ten days before Reichshoffen, and yet we suspected nothing ; our own little plans were enough for us, you see.

" I was in the country when the war was declared—out beyond Reichshoffen. I could not get back to Strasburg. I saw the last of the French driven down the road behind Elsasshausen—I have seen—*Mon Dieu !* what have I not seen in those ten days before I could get through the lines to Nancy ! I had an aunt there, and, can you imagine, when I reached Nancy at last it was August 16th, the day the Germans occupied the town, and my aunt had left for Paris the night before ! What could I do ? I went straight to the Red Lion, and asked for a room. They said there were no rooms ; there were fifty Germans there, and the officers were drinking in the dining-room and the landlady was hidden under her bed. I do not know what was in me that day ; it was seven o'clock, and I had had no food since morning, but I was strong and I had seen so much that I had no fear left.

" ' Why are the Germans allowed to carouse in the dining-room ? ' I asked. ' Who is the commanding officer ? '

" ' The Colonel is in No. 14,' blubbered the

garçon—they were all frightened out of their senses—' but no one dares disturb him, and I do not speak German.'

"I knew he lied about that, but I said, ' Show me No. 14! I speak German.'

"We rapped at the door. The Colonel came in his stocking feet and with a blanket wrapped around his shoulders ; he had had no rest for forty hours.

" ' I must have a room here in this inn,' said I, ' and I must sleep. I have come through the lines. Here is my pass. Your officers are drinking in the dining-room and terrifying the house. Can you not quiet them ? '

" He looked at me and swallowed a curse. Then, ' *Sie sind ein braves Mädchen,*' he cried, and ran downstairs, and the *garçon* and I were close behind him. He flung open the dining-room door. There were three young officers there, who had been drinking champagne since four o'clock. They too had had nothing to eat for a whole day. The empty champagne bottles were piled in a pyramid upon the table, and the men were quarrelling. Just as we opened the door the lieutenant with his back to us— with his back to us—struck his fellow-officer in the face. The Colonel saw it and he threw the door together behind him and thundered out an order, and left me standing outside. I did not see the blow given—it was the *garçon* who told me.

"I do not remember anything more, except a great drowsiness. I was at the end. I believe the *garçon* showed me to a room next the landlady's; I am not sure that I was not carried into it. But there I fell on the bed and slept; I did not even lock the door. I did not dream until just before I woke, and then I saw Friedrich sitting in a cloud of smoke with his back to me.

"The *garçon* was pounding on the door. He put his head in and saw me lying there.

"'You are ill?' said he.

"'No,' I answered.

"'Mademoiselle can have breakfast. The Badeners are gone long ago; they have been transferred to the Black Dog.'

"'*The Badeners?*' I cried.

"'You are ill, Mademoiselle,' he said.

"'No! *The Badeners?*'

"'Yes. They are all at the Black Dog— except the one with his back to us; the one we saw strike his friend.'

"'*And he?*' I leaped toward the door.

"'They have just shot him.'

.   .   .   .   .   .

"They shot him. He was my *fiancé*, and it was I that killed him, killed him in the war. Do you know what is in our hearts when you toast Alsace - Lorraine, Monsieur Merveille ? What can you know about 1870 ? You were only fourteen years old ! But I know."

Mademoiselle Aubépine had risen, and was grasping the end of the little table to steady herself. Her eyes seemed to be closed.

" That is why I am a singing-teacher. It is all over—forever—but I toast Alsace-Lorraine. Come, Monsieur Merveille."

She filled her glass and my own.

" To the dead," she said, in a hoarse whisper ; " *Austrinken !* "

Then she turned, gazed at me a moment with eyes from which the horror of that memory had not yet disappeared, and with a low, swift "*Pardon, Monsieur*," her black dress brushed by me in the twilight, and she was gone.

I never saw Mademoiselle Aubépine again. When I left in the morning, she had not come down from her room, and I thought the worthy innkeeper and his wife appeared somewhat troubled when I desired them to present my re-membrances to Mademoiselle. Perhaps they had fancied, between themselves, that the ac-quaintance of the young people would not end in remembrances merely. I do not know. But I know that all the way back to Strasburg the sight of the blood - red poppies in the green wheat made me shudder, and I fancied that everywhere in those lovely June fields, the *beau jardin*, as Louis XIV. called them long ago, I could trace the lines of battle-trenches; and the first thing I saw on climbing to my lodging in the Hennengasse and looking out of the window, was a Baden regiment marching by, filling the narrow street with their elastic onward motion, while the sun gleamed on their helmets and rifle-tips and yellow-skinned knapsacks in shifting lines and blotches of scaly gold, and the black shadows of the crooked street fell in bars across the glistening, sinuous, living mass, until it seemed like the undulation of a serpent.

Lombardy Poplars

LOMBARDY POPLARS

IT was very cool under the rock-maples in front of the Simpson place, and the Deacon, trudging up from the lower meadow in the dazzling July noon, eyed the shade irresolutely. He was trailing a rake behind him, and in front of him was a panting shepherd-dog.

" Deacon Simpson ! " called out a voice from one of the hammocks. " I want to ask you some more questions, Deacon Simpson."

The opportunity to oblige a boarder coincided remarkably with his own inclination to sit down, and the Deacon dropped into a comfortable position at the foot of the biggest maple. The rake was balanced upon his sharp old knees, and his blue overalls were drawn high above his ankles. He fanned himself slowly with his broad, green-lined linen hat.

" Yis, ma'am ? " he inquired benevolently. " Want to ask about another farm, don't ye, Miss Hertford ? "

The trim little woman in the hammock sat up straight. "How do you know I do?"

"Why, the women folks said you was off kind o' prospectin' round. Ruther hot, wa'n't it?"

"Oh, yes; I didn't mind. Didn't you tell me, Deacon Simpson, that the Dickinson place could be bought for four hundred dollars?"

"Wal, I guess it could," the Deacon assented, reflectively. "Jest look at that dog's tongue run out! Swelterin', ain't it, Jocko?"

But the Boston school-teacher was persistent. "And you said that other farm could be had for three hundred and fifty? The one where the barns are blown over."

"Wal, I shouldn't wonder if three hundred 'n' fifty in cash would come pretty near the sellin' price now. Mis' Simpson was raised on that farm."

"Really? I should think you would wish to keep it in the family, Deacon. But I've found another one that I like better than either of those."

"You don't say! Ain't bought it yet, have ye? Set still, Jocko!" He tapped the dog's back with the rakestale.

"No, I haven't bought it," said Miss Hertford, "but I really think I shall, if I can find the owner. Who is he? It's a story-and-half house with a great big chimney, about three-quarters of a mile from here on the county road. There's the loveliest old orchard back of the house, and a brook that runs through a stone-arched bridge, and a great swamp across the road, full of red-winged blackbirds. Do you suppose there are snakes in that swamp, Deacon?"

The prudent entertainer of summer boarders shook his head. "I never saw any there. Pretty scarce round here, anyway." He thoughtfully omitted to mention the "check'id adder" he had killed that morning in the lower meadow. "I dunno's I know which place you mean," he went on. "Is there an old shed jest across the road?"

"No, it's all open ground there, and from the doorstep you can look clear across the swamp and up to Oak Ridge, and at the right you can see all the hills beyond the Deerfield, and Greylock back of those. And there are two old Lombardy poplars in front of the house."

"Lumbuddy popples, eh? I want to know if you've ben clear up to Popple Hill! Wa'n't it awful hot for ye? I guess you must be talkin' about the old Jarvis place."

"The Jarvis place," Miss Hertford repeated, slowly. She rather liked the name. "Do you suppose it's for sale? It is entirely deserted. I went up and looked through the windows. Who is the owner?"

"They ain't a Jarvis in town," said the Deacon, deliberately. "Old Jedidiah Jarvis is dead, and Monroe Jarvis, he's dead. Young Frank Jarvis's wife died, and he went out West somewhere, and they say he's makin' money. He must own that place. He gets back here most every summer, 'n' stays jest about long enough to say 'How d'ye do?' and then he's off again. It was his grandfather that set out those popples; brought the shoots all the way from Philadelphy sewed into the linin' of his coat. Kind o' curis about Lumbuddy popples now; they do say that when you plant 'em in front of a house, the family sort o' dies out after a while. Last summer they was a professor up here who was tellin' me that popples hadn't any sect, or were all one sect, I forget which. That would make all the Lumbuddy popples in the *U*nited States jest the same age, ye see, all came by shoots from the fust one ever brought over from furrin parts. No wonder they get kind o' old 'n' run down, eh?"

Miss Hertford made no response to the Deacon's botanical fancies. "Do you suppose this Frank Jarvis would like to sell?" she interrupted. "How much land is there?"

But before the Deacon could finish his computation of wood-lot and mowing and pasture-land, the dinner-bell jingled viciously, and Miss Hertford, like a model boarder, abandoned her inquiries.

All the afternoon, however, she sat beneath the maples, meditating upon the Jarvis place. She even went so far as to write Madame Michel, the accomplished instructor of French at the Reverdy School, and her most intimate friend, that the deserted farm-house they had been in search of was found. It only remained to communicate with the owner and to make the necessary legal transfer; then they would be emancipated forever from Mis' Simpson's buckwheat-cake breakfasts, and the conversation of Mis' Simpson's other boarders, while still retaining all that was admirable in South Broughton as a summer home.

After tea she slipped out of the house, and crossing the Deacon's home pastures, climbed over the stone wall into the county road. In twenty minutes — not counting the time lost in picking red raspberries by the roadside and poking at the purple milk-weed blossoms with the tip of her parasol—she reached Poplar Hill, and stood again on the stone doorstep of the Jarvis place. The poplars rustled gently in the south wind; under the arch of the stone bridge the brook gurgled placidly; in the glen that bordered the swamp a wood-thrush was singing. Oak Ridge was still aglow with sunlight, but the wide intervales were already growing damp and cool, and the hills beyond the Deerfield were a deep, dull blue. It was lonely here, but it was the loneliness of peace.

Miss Hertford walked around the house twice, and then she tried the windows. The one nearest the front door was loosely fastened. She raised it without much difficulty, and profiting by her previous experience in exploring deserted farm-houses, reached around and unbolted the door. Glancing up and down the grass-grown road, she pulled the door open and slipped in, closing it after her. At the right was the living-room, with a large marble-sided fireplace, and an old-fashioned brick oven built into the chimney. Miss Hertford peered into the oven delightedly; she approved of every feature of the room, down to the round cat-hole in the foot-board by the chimney corner. This would be such a convenience for Madame Michel's Alexis, when they three should begin house-keeping ! On the left of the door was the parlor, and a bedroom leading from it. There was a kitchen and woodshed in the rear. Miss Hertford picked her way daintily over the whole house, upstairs and down ; she was by this time an adept in determining the soundness of timbers and the quality of floors, and in distinguishing the properly musty odor of a long-closed house from the mouldiness that comes from a damp cellar. The Jarvis house stood all tests triumphantly. It was perfectly clean and utterly empty ; there were no relics of wayfaring tramps or of haymakers' lunches, not even a rusty rat-trap nor an ancient almanac. The only article of any kind to be found in the house was a glass tumbler on the shelf of the bedroom, holding a few withered flowers, so shrivelled as to be unrecognizable.

While Miss Hertford stood looking at this old bouquet, she felt for the first time solitary and ill at ease in the deserted house. It was growing dark, too, and she went out somewhat hastily, bolting the door and closing the window. The light was gone from Oak Ridge now ; fireflies were sparkling in the swamp; the wind had risen, and the Lombardy poplars were creaking mournfully. They seemed unnaturally tall and rigid, so gaunt and barren in the

dusk, that Miss Hertford was reminded involuntarily of Deacon Simpson's comment; there
was something pathetic in their a-sexualism,
their sterile life which, nevertheless, outlived
the human generations that sprang up and
perished upon this infertile New England soil.
Miss Hertford shivered a little. She was thirty-
one years old, and alone in the world. In a
few years she would be as old as Madame
Michel—an old woman—the old story—so it
would go. She wished Madame Michel, that
cheery philosopher, were with her now, and
she walked rapidly down the darkening road
toward Deacon Simpson's.

But the next day this mood had passed. She
ascertained Frank Jarvis's Nevada address from
the postmistress—he was in the lumber business,
apparently—and directed to him what she considered a most business-like offer for the abandoned farm. Then she resigned herself to two
weeks' waiting, spending her mornings in preparing her new lectures in psychology for the
Reverdy School, and devoting most of her
afternoons to the Jarvis place. One day, in
rambling through the orchard above the house,
she found in the upper corner, under the shadow of a group of blighted plum-trees, a solitary grave. The burying-ground at South

Broughton was two miles away, and she was familiar enough with the isolated group of headstones that was to be seen near almost every farm, yet this discovery affected her in a way she could scarcely explain to herself. It seemed almost like sacrilege to offer to buy the place now. The gravestone bore a woman's name—Mary Rood Jarvis ; the birth-year was just that of Mary Hertford, and the woman, dying at twenty-one, had been dead ten years. The grass was high around the stone, and Miss Hertford plucked it away a little, and laid some daisies there. She would have liked to ask Deacon Simpson about this Mary Rood, wife of Frank Jarvis, but she shrank from doing so.

Two or three afternoons later she had a fright. She had walked up to the Jarvis place as usual, and had taken a fancy to go over the house again. As it happened, the last room she entered was the tiny bedroom, and there in the glass upon the shelf, instead of the withered bouquet of last year's blooming, was a handful of fresh iris flowers, such as grew by the brook below the house. For an instant her heart stopped beating ; then, as befitted a corresponding member of the Society for Psychical Research, she pressed her hands to her temples, steadied herself, and went up to them, to

test the class of illusory phenomena to which
they belonged. But they were no phantasm;
the blue petals were crisp and odorous, and,
caught in the hairy heart of one flower, an
insect was still struggling to get free. Having
done her professional duty, Miss Hertford fled,
like a well-bred woman who has unwittingly
found herself guilty of intrusion. Fresh flowers in that deserted chamber! Who could
have brought them there?

As Miss Hertford was hurriedly closing the
window, after having bolted the door on the
inside, a man came around the corner of the
house. He was whittling aimlessly at a branch
of lilac, and Miss Hertford, from over her
shoulder, caught the gleam of the open knife.
But she shut the window as calmly as she could,
and faced him. He shifted the knife to his
left hand, and took off his gray felt hat as
politely as was consistent with utter astonish-
ment. This slender, erect little woman, in
blue outing-suit and round sailor-hat, with honest eyes and wide forehead, a sketching-pad
and novel in her hands, was coolly making her
exit from his own house!

"How do you do?" he said, dryly. "My
name is Jarvis."

Thereupon Miss Hertford, standing on the

cracked marble doorstep, felt her face grow intolerably hot.

"Mr. Jarvis, I *beg* your pardon," she exclaimed. "I—I feel like a thief."

"Oh, you needn't," he replied. He had by this time classified her as a summer boarder. "There isn't much left to steal."

"No," she said, "nothing but——" Miss Hertford stopped awkwardly. She was thinking of the blue iris.

"I see you have learned how to get in," he added, as if trying to place her at her ease. "I thought I was the only one who understood the trick of that window."

"Please forgive me," she replied, abjectly. "Did you receive my letter?"

He stared at her. For a man who had been ten months in a lumber camp, Miss Hertford was a pleasant person to contemplate, and he made the most of his opportunity.

"I wrote you in Nevada some ten days ago," she explained. "I wanted—that is, Madame Michel and I wanted—to know whether you would sell this property. We were very anxious to buy it if we could—and that, Mr. Jarvis, is my only excuse, and I know it is a wretched one, for taking such liberties here."

Her apology seemed singularly unsatisfactory

to herself. He was so different from the lumberman to whom she had supposed she was writing. He was younger, for one thing—not yet thirty-five. His hands and face were deeply tanned, and his tawny mustache was bleached by the sun. The spare, sinewy figure was clad in a business-suit of the best San Francisco fashion. There was something distinguished about his slightly bald head, when he had taken off his hat. After all, was he the lumberman?

"This is Mr. Frank Jarvis, isn't it?" she inquired, in perplexity.

"Yes," he smiled. "But I did not receive your letter; I must have started East too soon. You have the advantage of me, Miss ——?"

"Miss Hertford. It is you, though, who have the advantage of me," she replied, playing upon his old-fashioned phrase. "Will you be generous and pardon the intrusion? I really had wished to buy the place very much." Miss Hertford's innocent fancies about the joy of the Westerner when he should receive her munificent offer of four hundred and seventy-five dollars for the farm and buildings had been suddenly dispelled.

"I don't think the place is for sale," he said, quietly.

Miss Hertford opened her red parasol, in

preparation for the hot walk back to Deacon Simpson's. Her dream of proprietorship was over. Frank Jarvis threw away his branch of lilac and pocketed his penknife.

" Mayn't I walk down with you?" he asked. "You are staying at the village, I suppose?"

"At Deacon Simpson's." She surrendered her parasol to him helplessly.

" I'm going to stop there to-night. The hotel is burned down, I believe."

"Yes."

As they passed under the shadow of the Lombardy poplars, Jarvis halted a moment and took a survey of the house. " It's a pretty spot," he said, slowly, "about the prettiest I ever saw anywhere. I always mean to get back here every summer, and see that the grass is mowed round the doorstep, and—up on the hill. I always open that window, too, and go inside. We began housekeeping in this old place, began—and ended." He stopped abruptly. The teacher of psychology pitied him.

" Those poplars don't look a day older than they did ten years ago, and they were old scraggy trees then," he continued, as they moved on again. "I don't know but they ought to come down. What do you think?"

Miss Hertford expressed herself somewhat

vaguely upon this point, and they started down the county road together, in the hot afternoon sun.

.   .   .   .   .   .

Frank Jarvis stayed ten days at the Deacon's, waiting, as he said, for business letters. Mis' Simpson affirmed after the first day that he was "sidlin' up" to Mary Hertford. But the "Professor," as Miss Hertford was commonly called at Simpson's, in recognition of the fact that the occupant of the chair of Mental and Moral Science at the Reverdy School was no ordinary schoolma'am, was herself not only oblivious of this rumor, but unaware of any grounds for it. She continued to work away steadily in the mornings: she finished her lecture on Consciousness of Self, recast her old notes upon Hypnotism, and began to take new ones on the Psychology of Dreams. She was scrupulously courteous to Mr. Jarvis, as she endeavored to be toward all her fellow-boarders, but Madame Michel, who had just joined her, really did the lion's share of entertaining the lumberman. He would sit by the Madame's hammock under the maples for hours at a time, amused by her social observations and occupying himself pleasantly by stimulating her romantic appetite for stories of Western life. His experiences were always

related in a slow, unvaried tone, with a mixt-
ure of New England reticence and Nevada pict-
uresqueness of phrase that Madame Michel
found extremely fascinating. She was never
tired of talking to Miss Hertford about it, and
sometimes, when Mr. Jarvis joined the two
ladies on their afternoon walks, Miss Hertford
seemed to enjoy his companionship. He was a
new species, and she analyzed him with a decorous interest. At least, that was the only
attitude toward him that, in Madame Michel's
opinion and to her disappointment, Miss Hertford ever seemed to take.

Yet it was Deacon Simpson, after all, who
seemed to get the most unalloyed delight from
Frank Jarvis's society. That a South Broughton boy, whose home had been broken up by
his wife's death when he was twenty-two, should
knock around half-a-dozen States and fail in as
many enterprises, and finally end by organizing
a lumber and fluming company, buying a tract
of pine land and a wrecked railroad leading to
it, hiring huge squads of Chinamen to get out
the timber, then shipping it into Virginia City
to be used for braces in the mines, and all at
a clear profit — as South Broughton people
affirmed—of forty or fifty thousand dollars a
year, seemed to the Deacon little less than a

miracle. After supper, when the boarders lingered for a while on the front piazza, Deacon
Simpson invariably endeavored to "dror Frank
Jarvis out," and prided himself upon his skill
in accomplishing his purpose. No less than
three times, to as many different groups, was
Jarvis forced to relate the one really thrill-
ing incident of his career as superintendent
of the lumber company, which had occurred
when a horde of angry Chinamen, led on by
a drunken overseer, had attempted to take
summary vengeance on the superintendent for
his vigor in breaking up gambling in the
logging camp. Jarvis told his story quietly
enough, but it made him a hero in the Deacon's eyes, and even Miss Hertford acknowledged to Madame Michel afterward, that there
was something fine in the man's courage at
his lonely post, and something very admirable
in his modesty.

When Jarvis went away, he bade Miss Hertford good-by under the maple-trees, at two
o'clock in the afternoon. Mis' Simpson, who
was watching them from behind the pantry
blinds, in the L part, was profoundly disappointed at this prosaic leave-taking. They
stood for several minutes together, Miss Hertford's hammock between them. Madame Mi-

chel had gone to her room in search of an auto-
graph-album, for Jarvis's signature, but it was
undoubtedly at the very bottom of her trunk,
since she delayed her return. The stage-driver
grew impatient, and finally Jarvis was obliged
to leave his regards for Madame Michel with
Miss Hertford. Then he put out his hand.
He had never before referred to the circumstances of their first meeting.

"It was a good moment for me when I saw
you come out of my own door," he said. "It
ought not to be the last time, ought it? Good-
by, Mary."

Was it embarrassment, or audacity, that made
him say that? Miss Hertford lay awake all
night trying to decide. Once or twice she
comforted herself by imagining that he was too
embarrassed to be aware of what he was saying,
only to be alarmed by the reflection that he
certainly did not seem embarrassed in the least.
His gray eyes had looked fixedly at her—so
fixedly, indeed, that she was conscious that her
own had failed to meet them. Miss Hertford
sat down to her books the next morning in a
state of singular helplessness, considering that
she was an expert in mental processes and had
just copied her lecture on Consciousness of Self,
and that she wanted nothing in life so much as

the opportunity to take a Ph.D. in Psychology at Leipsic.

. . . .

One dreary evening in the following February she had a letter from Frank Jarvis. The yellow envelope, with the name of the lumber and fluming company stamped upon it, had been directed to her in care of Deacon Simpson. It had been two or three weeks upon the way, and she could not help imagining that Mis' Simpson had opened it over a tea-kettle and had cunningly stuck it together again. There was nevertheless nothing in the letter which Mis' Simpson might not have been permitted to read. Its general theme was the severity of the winter at the logging camp. The stage-road had been broken through that day for the first time in six weeks, and the superintendent's only connection with the outer world had been his telephone wire to Checkerberry City. He had pushed over the Divide a couple of times on snow-shoes for his mail, but the drifts were so soft that it was risky work. Five of his wood-choppers had been lost in the snow since Christmas Eve, and but one body had been found, though he had been out for days, following every coyote track for miles around. His men were getting restless; some rascal had sledded a cask of whiskey over the Divide, and he could not discover in which cabin it was hidden. The Chinamen were sulky. He had had to break up their gambling games again. It was rather lonesome business keeping the whip - hand over three hundred men, but there was no help for it. He was thankful enough to have his telephone ; he did not see how he could have held out without that. But now that the stage-route was open once more, all would go well, he hoped. Indeed, he thought he could get down to San Francisco in two or three days more, and in that case, business might summon him East. If he came, might he call upon her ? It would give him great pleasure—the very greatest pleasure—to do so. And he sent his regards to Madame Michel.

Miss Hertford did not deliver this last message to her friend. Madame Michel had teased her about Mr. Jarvis all the autumn, but since then had not mentioned his name. The northeast wind shook savagely at the window of Miss Hertford's room, on the third floor of the Reverdy School, while she read and re-read Frank Jarvis's letter. It was not a love-letter —not a love-letter—she kept repeating to herself, and yet she locked the door of the little room as if it were. The solitariness of his life came home to her as never before. She pictured the winter camp in Nevada, with that isolated figure in the midst of it, toiling as gallantly as if life's best trophies were still to be gained, bravely forgetful of the early wreck his happiness had suffered. She pitied him, as she had not pitied him since the afternoon in South Broughton, when he had spoken of his early home, and the girl-wife resting in that upland orchard. He must be terribly lonely out there; she believed she would write him some day a cheery letter. There would be no harm in that. She herself knew what it was to be lonely; indeed, she was very lonely to-night, with the wind roaring around the Reverdy building and piling the wet snow against the panes, while her one intimate friend, Madame Michel, sat in her cosey parlor on the other floor, before an open fire, stroking Alexis's back. Poor Madame Michel; she too had had her glimpse of happiness, but that was long ago, and now she made the best of what was left to her. So it went in this world—one person here, another there— the figures in the pattern do not match—if only the kaleidoscope were shaken a little differently!

Then her breath came quick. What should she say to Frank Jarvis if he called? She felt

sure he would come ; she knew why he was
coming ; it was because he loved her. She
was sure of it the moment she saw that yellow
envelope. What could she say ? Louder swept
the storm around her corner of the Reverdy
School ; higher mounted the snow upon the
window-sill. It wrought nervously upon her.
Her mind failed to obey orders—a sort of terror
took possession of her. When she went to bed,
at last, she turned back, after extinguishing the
gas, and taking Jarvis's letter, put it under her
pillow.

Yet the school-teaching consciousness is slow
to lose its hold, and even while her hand rested
upon his letter, she thought of her morrow's
work. The psychology class, now in wild enthusiasm over the phenomena of dreaming, had
all agreed to think of some object before falling asleep, and to report their dreams in the
morning. The teacher, too, had promised to
experiment and report. Too tired to direct the
stream of her own thought, it now bore her
back out of the February storm to summer days
in South Broughton, and to long afternoons
spent at the Jarvis place. The shadow of the
Lombardy poplars still fell across the marble
doorstep — the tall, homely trees, patiently
watching the inhabitants of the Jarvis place

born and married and buried, secure in their
own self-perpetuated, sexless life. Two deso-
late trees on a lonely hilltop, isolated from all
their kind, but peaceful none the less—their
leaves whitening in this gentle July wind—such
quiet old Lombardy poplars—so—quiet— And
Miss Hertford was asleep.

Toward morning she awoke from a dream so
vivid that conscious life seemed pale when con-
fronted with it. A hot wind was blowing over
fields full of ripening grass and ox-eyed daisies,
over a swamp where sweet-flag waved and a
few late blue iris flowers lingered, and over an
upland orchard of gnarled apple-trees where
golden-winged woodpeckers nested, only that
the birds were all blown away now by the
wind. Fiercer and hotter grew the gale: it
twisted the brittle dead limbs from a pair of
gaunt Lombardy poplars ; it swayed them back
and forth and beat them together till both came
crashing down ; then from out the torn and in-
termingling branches strange flowers started
into bloom—heavy-odored and so white ! The
fallen trees were covered with them as with
snow ; no, it *was* snow—snow everywhere—filling all the intervale away over to Oak Ridge,
only Oak Ridge was ten times higher than she
had ever seen it, and the intervale was full of

giant pines. Log-cabins were scattered here
and there, and out of them streamed throngs of
Chinamen, headed by drunken overseers. All
were converging upon a single house—their
steps were noiseless in the snow, and the wind,
grown icy-cold now, drowned their voices, but
the moonlight glittered on axe-blades and pis-
tol-barrels. A lamp flashed in the solitary
house, and instantly the dark masses of men
made a rush for it, swarming at the door, the
window, even on the roof; then a sudden panic
seemed to seize them, for they drew off again,
except two that lay by the door, black and mo-
tionless in the moonlight. It was Frank Jarvis
there inside. He had barricaded the door with
a roller-top desk, and had stuffed a mattress into the lower half of the window. He was but
partly dressed; there was an ugly look in his
gray eyes, and he held a smoking revolver. He
was calling up Checkerberry City by telephone,
with the same slow voice as ever : " I want a sher-
iff's posse up here right away. Trouble with
the Chinamen. Say—John—if anything hap-
pens to me, I wish you would forward a message
to Miss Mary Hertford, care of Deacon Simpson, South Broughton, Massachusetts. Got it?
Tell her I send my love, and ask her——" But
down came door and window under the rush

of axe-blows; the furious black stream poured in upon him. It was like a swarm of bees—black—black. The wind died, and she woke.

It was twenty-three minutes past five. Miss Hertford, in all the strange horror of that moment, noted the fact instinctively, and calculated the time-difference between Boston and Nevada. She did not doubt that Frank Jarvis was dead, nor that his death had been instantaneously made known to her by the mysterious processes of telepathy. There were hundreds of such cases on record in the books upon her table. She herself had collected half a dozen, and forwarded them to the Society for Psychical Research. It was not strange to her that she had been made aware of his death, but it seemed pitifully strange that she should have grown conscious of her love for him at the very moment when it was too late. For she knew, now, that she loved him; indeed, she was not sure that she had not loved him, all unknown to herself, from the day when they walked home from Poplar Hill together.

The Reverdy girls counted Miss Hertford's gray hairs that morning, for the first time. She seemed to herself, as well as to others, like an old woman. Madame Michel, startled at the utter misery in her face and demeanor, tried by intervals all the forenoon to pet her, to win out of her the reason of her trouble. She even had her arm about Miss Hertford's waist, in school-girl fashion, when the two teachers came down to their twelve o'clock recitations. Miss Hertford's young ladies, in a tumult of excitement over their dreams, were waiting for her in the room at the left of the front door. The door-bell rang, and Madame Michel, disengaging her arm, answered it herself. Miss Hertford was crossing the threshold of her recitation-room, when she heard an exclamation behind her.

" Mr. Jarvees ! " Madame Michel cried again. " Enter, if you please ; you are the very welcome ! " She ushered him in excitedly. He smiled radiantly at her. One side of his face and mustache was wet with snow ; he shook it apologetically from his fur overcoat. Then he caught sight of Miss Hertford, and in an instant was in front of her, holding out both hands. She was white and trembling ; the effort to raise her hand to his gave her physical torture ; she murmured his name incoherently. Madame Michel drew aside the curtains of the reception-room, conscious that the psychology class was studying the situation through the crack of the door.

"You do not arrive from South Broughton, Mr. Jarvees?" she inquired, feeling that somebody ought to say something.

"Oh, yes," replied Jarvis, forgetting to relinquish Miss Hertford's hand, as he half-led, half-followed her into the reception-room. "I stayed at Deacon Simpson's last night. I can tell you the wind blew up there! This morning, Miss Hertford, as we drove by the old place, the Lombardy poplars were blown down."

Mary Hertford looked up at him; the color mounted in her cheeks till they were rosy red; she lifted her free hand helplessly to the other —to his; and Madame Michel quietly drew the portière together again, murmuring all to herself a triumphant "*Enfin!*"

Then she crossed the hall to Miss Hertford's recitation-room. "Young ladies," she announced, with as nearly perfect an assumption of her dry school-room tone as was possible to her at that moment, "the class in Pseechologee is dismeessed!"

The Phenix

THE PHENIX

I.

"COUNTESS, may I trouble you for that cauliflower?"

The Countess's eyes were hovering restlessly about the farther end of the long *pension* table, but she recollected herself instantly at the sound of this mandatory voice at her right.

"Certainly, Frau Lieutenant," she exclaimed. "Pardon me;" and as the servant was still busy at the other extremity of the room, she lifted the nearly empty platter and passed it.

The Frau Lieutenant surveyed the cauliflower with an eye trained by twenty-five years of experience at table-d'hôte dinners. The selection of fricasseed chicken was her specialty, though there was not a woman in Berlin who could be more implicitly trusted to secure the best piece of anything the first time trying; but really the cauliflower offered no opportunity for her skill. There was but one bunch still untouched, and she divided this into two exactly equal portions.

"Letty, my dear," she said in English, balancing one of these portions upon the spoon, "take this."

"But, Mammachen," protested Miss Letty, a slender, delicate-complexioned girl of twenty-three, "I don't——"

"Take it, my dear," said the Frau Lieutenant, imperturbably, depositing the cauliflower by the side of the stewed mutton on her daughter's plate, and rapidly assisting herself to the remaining portion. "It is very fattening."

This last was in a tone intended for a whisper, but the Frau Lieutenant Dettmar's strident voice had a remarkably penetrating quality, and an under-sized Englishman, who sat directly opposite Miss Dettmar, looked up at the words. He was near-sighted, and the dining-room of the Countess von Eckmüller's *pension* was never brilliantly illuminated, especially on a dingy winter afternoon. It was only two o'clock, but the murky fog was already settling down into the Dorotheen Strasse, and the corners of the high, ugly room were growing dusky. The Englishman peered across the table curiously at his two countrywomen, for such did the mother and daughter unmistakably appear to be. Stubbworth's insight into character, like his visual faculty, was not of the keenest, but he could not help noting the difference between the muscular, assertive body of Mrs. Dettmar, her square, red face, with combative black eyes overtopped by a blacker false front of hair, and the slightly stooping figure of Miss Letty, with her light-blue child's eyes, the vague pink of her cheeks, and the shyness with which she pecked with her fork at the cauliflower. The daughter had evidently the physical characteristics of her father, the lamented Lieutenant Dettmar. So Stubbworth reflected, as the result of his inspection, and wished that he might address the girl in English ; but not daring to transgress the Countess's rule that only German should be spoken at meal-times, he let his spectacled eyes fall to his plate again, began to separate the bones out of his mutton stew, and to meditate upon his forthcoming edition of " Middle English Homilies," the preparation of which had brought him to Berlin.

The lower end of the table, where sat the students and the commercial young men, was uproarious, as usual. A Jewess—studying for the opera—who sat at Stubbworth's left, laughed once or twice at a student witticism so immoderately, that the sedate Englishman was embarrassed, but the effervescing humor lost its sparkle by the time it reached the neighborhood of the

Countess. The people there were dull. The Widow Dettmar's soup had been cold, she had lost the first chance at the stew, and she ate away morosely. The Countess said nothing, but glanced from time to time toward the empty plate at her left, and once she whispered an order to the servant. By and by the Jewess turned her dark face toward the head of the table.

"Countess von Eckmüller," she asked, "is not Herr Jarlson coming to-day?"

"Certainly," was the answer. "He was called at half-past one, as usual."

"At half-past one!" interrupted the Frau Lieutenant Dettmar. "You don't mean to say that that young man——"

"Exactly," said the Countess. "He is called at half-past one. If he does not get up by a quarter to two, I take one of his shoes, I open his door, and I cry 'Hamlet! Arise!' and toss the shoe at him. Then he gets up."

"I never heard of such a thing," cried the Englishwoman. "Did you, Letty, my dear?"

"No, Mammachen," replied Miss Letty, "but it is very funny."

"It is very irregular," said Mrs. Dettmar, severely. "He is a wild young man. One does not have to look at him twice to know that."

" No, Frau Lieutenant," remarked the Countess, " you misunderstand Herr Jarlson completely. It is only his way."

" Yes, his way. I know men. When a young actor sits in the cafés till four o'clock in the morning, and that every night in the week, and sleeps half the day, of course he is wild. He must be. Oh, I know ! It's better for him to have his fling, though ; he'll settle down when he is thirty. My husband used to say to me that those men were always steady afterward. They make the best husbands. As I told Letty the other day——"

" Mammachen," pleaded Miss Letty, crimsoning.

But the widow's worldly philosophy was cut short. A door opened half - way down the room, and a tall young fellow entered, apologetically. Everyone looked up.

" Here he comes," cried the Countess, with a smile on her shrewd old face. " He has risen, like—like—why, he is my Phenix."

There was a chorus of laughter. " The Phenix ! The Phenix ! " echoed from the students, as Herr Jarlson took his seat at the Countess's left. There was indeed something eagle-like in the curve of his nose, and the stiff masses of his hair, brushed à la Pompadour, seemed curiously like a bird's crest. "The Phenix," chuckled the Countess again to herself, delighted at her own fantasy.

"Letty, my dear," whispered Mrs. Dettmar in English, to her daughter, "what is a Phenix?"

"I think, Mammachen," was the doubtful answer, murmured behind a handkerchief, lest the new-comer opposite should hear, "I think it was a bird. Anyway, it rose."

The Norwegian, bowing respectfully to the English ladies, proceeded to open a bottle of beer, which the Countess provided at dinner for each of her numerous family, and to empty it bodily into a huge silver goblet that stood beside his plate. It was very bad beer, in truth, but Herr Jarlson always maintained it was delicious in his Scandinavian goblet. He took a draught of it now, before unrolling his napkin, and then turning to the Countess he exclaimed, enthusiastically: "It was grand!"

"Do you mean the beer, Herr Jarlson?" demanded Mrs. Dettmar, with veiled irony.

The Phenix lifted his gray eyes to the widow's face. He had a proper terror of her, a terror not diminished by his secret admiration of her daughter.

"No, not this time," he replied, in fluent German. "It was the 'Ghosts.'"

"The ghosts? What do you mean? Do you see ghosts all the forenoon, after coming in at four o'clock in the morning?" The widow was so amused at her joke that she did not hear Miss Letty whispering that Herr Jarlson meant a play.

"It was Ibsen's 'Ghosts,' Frau Lieutenant," explained the Countess, quietly, "given at the Residenz Theatre yesterday."

"Ah," said the widow. She was not interested in such matters.

"It was a feast to my soul," Herr Jarlson went on; "almost as good as hearing it in Norwegian again."

"You must tell me all about it later," said Countess von Eckmüller. That was the first representation of "Ghosts" in Berlin, and it had not yet become fashionable to discuss the play at dinner.

"Herr Jarlson," spoke up the Jewess, "did you remember?"

"Certainly, Fräulein," and the Phenix unbuttoned his frock-coat and pulled out a complimentary ticket to "Siegfried," which he asked Stubbworth to pass to her. She thanked him so effusively that he forgot to mention that the ticket for which she had applied through him had really not been granted, and that he had presented her with his own instead. As an accredited student of acting and a fellow of some promise in his calling Herr Jarlson's name stood higher on the complimentary lists than did hers.

It was curious to see how the Norwegian's appearance changed the atmosphere of the upper end of the table. The Countess became chatty. The servant brought a new dish of cauliflower, expressly kept hot for Herr Jarlson, but Mrs. Dettmar had a helping from it, and was thereby put in good spirits again. Miss Letty glanced across the table timidly, from time to time, and wondered why the Phenix did not brush his hair like other people; he was such an odd young man. She fancied how he would look with a mustache—such a mustache, for instance, as had Major Vischer, her formal engagement to whom was to be announced next week, at Christmas. The Major had a luxuriant growth upon his upper lip, but Miss Letty somehow wished he were not so bald; she would almost rather have his hair stand on end, like Herr Jarlson's. Then Miss Letty blushed to think what Mammachen would say if she knew her daughter had ventured to criticise the estimable Major Vischer. The Major had been so kind, and her ring next

week would be no cheap little German affair,
she was quite sure. Mammachen was right, of
course; a husband of forty—even if he were
bald and fat—was forty times better than no
husband; and the Major was so kind; and
yet——

But Mammachen was talking about Christmas, with the Countess and Herr Jarlson.
"No, they should be useful," she was saying,
in her polemic voice. "The idea of sending
flowers as a gift! They wither in two days,
and it is money thrown away. If anybody
sent me flowers, I should be mad."

The Countess nodded assent, having kept a
pension too long to differ unnecessarily with
her patrons; but what she was thinking of was
this: "Send flowers to you? *Ich danke.* I
should be more likely to send you a roast-beef
rare."

"I remember the first present Lieutenant
Dettmar ever gave me," continued the widow.
"It was a book, and I have it yet; whereas,
you see, if it had been flowers, I should have
had to throw them away the day after. My
husband was so sensible. Letty, my dear,
what was that book that Papa gave me?"

"It was 'Proverbs of All Nations,' Mammachen."

As Miss Letty gave this information, she was conscious that both Jarlson and Stubbworth were looking at her. She thought that a certain whimsical expression passed over the Norwegian's thin lips, and she blushed again. She was very timid.

The conversation turned to other subjects, but as for the Phenix, he continued to meditate upon these countrywomen of Shakespeare until the dinner was over, and then he pushed back his chair, opened another bottle of beer, and began to talk with the Countess about the third act of Ibsen's " Ghosts."

II.

IT was five o'clock in the morning, the day
before Christmas. Outside, in the Dorotheen Strasse, it was bitter cold. The *droschke*
drivers on night service slapped their arms and
shivered on their boxes, and the tramway horses
staggered on the slippery frost as the huge
double-decked cars swung groaning around the
curve by the Countess von Eckmüller's *pension*.
In Stubbworth's tiny bedroom on the third
floor, it was not much warmer. The tall por-
celain stove was polished and white like a
tombstone, and fully as cold. The Englishman had already risen and was seated by his
lamp, wrapped in a blanket dressing-gown,
and with a towel around his forehead. He
was turning the leaves of a huge Latin folio
from the Royal Library, and making annota-
tions. His edition of Homilies had been almost ready, poor fellow, when a German pub-
lished the startling suggestion that the English
monk who wrote them was indebted for some

of his ideas to the Latin sermons of a certain Dutch bishop of the thirteenth century, whereupon Stubbworth had secured a month's respite from his duties as private tutor in the family of a Norfolk nobleman, and had spent half his year's savings in a trip to Berlin, in order to investigate the extent of the monk's obligation to his worthy Dutch contemporary. The laborious comparison promised to be singularly barren of results, but Stubbworth had the comfort of knowing that, provided his methods were sufficiently painstaking, his chances of securing a Ph.D. were not invalidated by the worthlessness of his conclusions.

It was with a slight feeling of annoyance at an interruption that Stubbworth paused in his task and listened to a footstep coming down the corridor. He knew it well, for it was the habit of the Phenix to study his rôles in the early morning, after getting home from the *Kneipe* and before going to bed, and many a time in the preceding three weeks had Stubbworth been wakened by the actor's coming in to borrow his Shakespeare, or to ask puzzling questions about the mounting of Irving's plays.

"Come in," grumbled Stubbworth, in answer to the knock; and then he was ashamed of his inhospitality, for he had been ill the day be-

fore and Jarlson had sat by him the whole afternoon, trying to amuse him by showing a collection of Scandinavian coins, and by telling
about student life at the university of Christiania.

The door opened quietly, and the Phenix
entered, his latch-key still in his hand. He
unbuttoned his pelisse, threw his fur cap upon
the bed, and sat down, dejectedly. " Do you
not feel better, Mr. Stubbworth ? " he asked.

" Something of a headache," said the Englishman, " but I think I shall work it off.
And you ? "

The actor shrugged his shoulders. " I am
freezing, for one thing. May I light a cigarette ? "

As Jarlson rolled it, Stubbworth noticed that
his fingers, which were of extraordinary length
and delicacy, were blue with cold.

" Have you been in the *Kneipe* till now ? "
asked Stubbworth, handing him a match.

" Till three o'clock," was the answer. " It
was stupid, to-night. And since then I have
been walking the streets. I suppose, if I had
been a practical Englishman, I should have had
my gloves with me." He tossed the burned
match toward the stove, and settled back
gloomily into his chair again, muttering an im-

precation upon Berlin tobacco. Stubbworth watched him silently, not having sufficient conversational command of German to say exactly what he thought. "What did you walk the streets for?" he finally asked.

"Without doubt, because I was a fool. All men are fools in Berlin; read what Heine says about it. Do you know Major Vischer?"

"I have seen him here. Miss Dettmar's—— ?"

"Yes, the betrothed of Mees Letty. We were both in the Café Bauer last evening; I had been reading the *Fliegende Blätter* and it lay on my table. He sent a waiter for it—and I handed it to the waiter." This last clause was in a stage tone that made Stubbworth smile.

"Well?" said he.

"But I should have flung it in the Major's face," cried Jarlson, fiercely, "and then two hours from now we should have been standing over on the Hasenheide, waiting for the word. Would you have been my second? I would have wanted you there to tell Mees Letty afterward."

"God forbid!" exclaimed Stubbworth. "The Major would have brought you down like a partridge, and it would have broken Miss Letty's heart."

" Do you think she would really care ? "

" Of course she would care, you silly fellow," growled Stubbworth, affectionately. " Do you think any girl with an English mother wants to have a duel fought about her ? She is to be formally engaged to the Major to-morrow, is she not ? Do you suppose she would want to marry a man who had just killed you ? " Stubbworth had very rarely put together as much German as that at a time, and was rather proud of it.

The Phenix tossed away his cigarette, and thrusting his shivering fingers deep into the pockets of his pelisse, dropped his chin upon his breast.

" You would better go to bed and get warm," continued Stubbworth, virtuously, " if you have had nothing better to think of than fighting Major Vischer, while you were walking Unter den Linden."

" But I had ! " exclaimed the young fellow, eagerly. " Much of the time I was thinking about her."

Stubbworth shut his Latin folio, and pushed his chair around to face Herr Jarlson. There were no love episodes in the " Middle English Homilies," and he felt ill at ease in his rôle of confidant.

"I was thinking of Mees Letty," Jarlson went on, "and the air was all like spring. Is she not beautiful?"

"Why, yes," admitted Stubbworth, wondering at the Norseman's simplicity.

"Do you think she would accept a gift from me to-day, the day before she is betrothed?"

Stubbworth stared at him. "A gift?"

"It is only a philopena. I lost it to her at dinner yesterday. But I did not think the Frau Mamma wished me to pay, and I did not know the English customs. She is really an English girl, you know, in spite of her German father and her continental life. Must I send her gloves?"

"Why, no," said Stubbworth, hesitatingly. "I don't see why you can't give her anything you like, if you fairly owe it."

"Very good;"—Jarlson's hands came out of his pockets with an inquiring gesture—"and now, could I give her a book?"

"I should think so; why can't you put it on the Christmas-tree to-night?"

The Phenix sprang to his feet. He was blessed with a volatile temperament, and notwithstanding his tragic designs of the past night, he had the healthy courage of his twenty-four years. He struck his hand into Stubbworth's just as *Don Carlos* greets the *Marquis of Posa.* " Mr. Stubbworth," he cried, " if I had had a' confidant like you six weeks ago, when I first met her, all might have been different. I do not understand the English ways ; I have not dared address her, and I have been afraid of the Mammachen. But now I will put that book upon the Christmas-tree in spite of all the Majors in Prussia, and if she thanks me for it, I will tell her in English——"

" You had better put it in German," interrupted Stubbworth, grimly.

" *Bewahre !* It shall either be in her mother tongue or in mine ; she knows not a word of Norwegian, and I shall say to her in English, ' *I atore you !* ' If she is angry, you will find me lying out on the Hasenheide in the morning."

And nodding his head sententiously at the astonished Englishman, who had not taken the actor's devotion to Miss Letty quite seriously enough, Herr Jarlson gathered his pelisse about him, and bowed himself grandly out of the bedroom door, in what would have been an admirable stage exit, had he not backed into a frightened servant, hurrying along the narrow corridor to start the kitchen fire. As for Mr.

Stubbworth, he stood a full minute looking at the door, before he found breath enough to grumble out something to himself about love being blind. But it was chillier in his room than it had seemed before, and he lighted his pipe and wasted ten minutes in a dull dream of something that had happened in his own undergraduate days. Then he wiped his spectacles, knotted the towel more closely around his forehead, tightened the belt of his old dressing-gown, and found his place again in the Latin folio.

III

A T six o'clock that evening the whole *pen-sion*, with a single exception, was gathered in the long dining-room. Through the crack in the folding - doors at one end, there could be seen the green and gilt of the Christmas - tree, which had been selected by the Countess herself at the *Jahrmarkt* the night before. The beloved Crown Prince Frederick, wandering with his younger children through the *Jahrmarkt* also—and, as it sadly proved, for the last time—had stopped in admiration before this very tree, though they had finally decided that it was not quite tall enough. But the incident was sufficient to add to the aroma of the fir a sort of odor of royalty.

There had been a remarkably good dinner at four o'clock, but now the table was cleared, save for a huge punch - bowl in the middle. Several toasts had been drunk already, and there were plenty more to come, for the tree was not to be lighted until eight o'clock. Each member of the miscellaneous family was pledged

183

to do something for the common entertainment, and the Countess began, bringing out a dusty harp from behind the sideboard, and playing fantasies in a fashion which made it easy for her audience to believe that the harp had resounded in the Countess's ancestral halls upon the Oder for immemorial centuries. Frau Lieutenant Dettmar, who was sceptical about the antiquity of the Countess's title, was unfortunately not in the dining-room. The postman had brought her some letters, just as dinner was over, and she had retired to her own room to read them. She did not come back. A medical student from Madrid danced a Spanish dance amid thunderous applause, and a toast was drunk to Spain ; but Mrs. Dettmar was still absent. Miss Letty, arrayed in her last season's Homburg finery, played, in the most modest and pretty way imaginable, her whole repertory of five pieces upon the guitar, and a toast was drunk to her native land ; but Mammachen was not there to see. Mr. Stubbworth, under the mellowing warmth of the occasion, delivered, in broken German, an impressive homily upon the intimate relations of England with Germany, and the students insisted upon toasting England once more ; and still Mrs. Dettmar sat in her room, reading those two letters.

The first was from a retired Prussian officer, an old friend of her husband. Presenting his apologies for referring to a matter so delicate, and alleging as his excuse his deep interest in the family of the late Lieutenant Dettmar, the writer made bold to inquire, in view of the approaching betrothal, whether the Frau Lieutenant was aware that Major Vischer, so far from being the man of property he was reputed, was, as a matter of fact, considerably in debt? Knowing that a mere word upon this subject would be sufficient to impress upon such a prudent mother the importance of an exact understanding of the financial condition of her future son-in-law, the writer begged leave to subscribe himself her very humble servant and the devoted friend of her lamented husband.

In debt? Major Vischer in debt? Major Vischer, who had served under her Franz in that Holstein business and again in the Austrian campaign ; who had sowed his wild oats long ago ; who owned, as she supposed, that fine estate in Saxony, and who was devoted to Miss Letty—Major Vischer actually in debt! The valiant widow trembled, like a rider who pulls up on the verge of a precipice. She had almost made the one blunder of her life !

The second letter was from the Major himself. He was chagrined to inform her that his duties as staff-officer suddenly called him away from Berlin that day, to inspect the fortress of Königstein. In vain had he pleaded with his superiors the importance of his family engagement ; they had been inexorable, and the morrow, to which he had looked forward with such ardent anticipation, would behold him in Saxon-Switzerland. He hoped to return by Sylvester Evening, the 31st, and he trusted that his dearest Miss Letty would consider New Year's Day as propitious a time for their betrothal as Christmas Day would have proved, had it not been for the stern duties of his profession.

Mrs. Dettmar breathed a little easier on reading this. Providence had come to her help, she was sure. There was a whole week in which to break to her daughter the dreadful news of the Major's poverty, and to prepare her for the inevitable rupture. Miss Letty worshipped the Major ! It would nearly break the dear child's heart, but that could not be helped. No girl of hers should ever marry a man who had misrepresented his income ! Still, she could not bear to spoil Letty's Christmas-eve.

She went back into the dining-room. The Jewess was just ending an aria from " Norma,"

amid rapturous expressions of delight. Then
there was a moment's awkwardness. Tolerant
as was this cosmopolitan *pension*, it could hardly be expected that anyone would propose a
toast to the Hebrews. But Herr Jarlson was
equal to the emergency.

"Gentlemen and ladies," he cried, "in
token of our appreciation of Fräulein Gold-
schmidt's talent, I propose that we drink to
the glory of Art!"

"Bravo!" called out the Countess.

Miss Letty clapped her little hands enthusiastically ; it had been so quick-witted in Herr
Jarlson ; not even the Major could have shown
a kinder heart. Mrs. Dettmar, who had taken
the seat reserved for her between the Countess
and Stubbworth, and at some little distance, as
it happened, from Miss Letty, joined with the
rest in the formal homage to Art. Then there
were loud calls for the Phenix, from all over
the room : "Play something for us!" "Herr
Jarlson!" "Herr Jarlson!" and some of those
who knew the rôles he had been studying,
cried, "Uriel Acosta!" and others, "Der
Prinz von Homburg!" The Phenix glanced
inquiringly at the Countess.

"You must obey, my Hamlet," she said,
"but you shall take whatever rôle you please."

He rose, buttoned his coat, and passed to the farther end of the room, where the students made place for him.

"It will be nothing improper, will it?" whispered Mrs. Dettmar.

"No," answered the Countess, sharply. "He is innocent as a child. He is thoroughly good ; he is not so much of a worldling as you or I, Frau Lieutenant. His late hours and his *Künstlerleben* are nothing but boyishness."

"Gentlemen and ladies," said the Phenix, "I shall have the honor of reciting from the first act of ' Don Carlos,' where the *Prince* confesses to the *Marquis of Posa* his love for the *Queen.*"

His face was pale and his voice husky. Instead of sleeping, that forenoon, he had been the round of the Berlin book-stores. There was a hush all through the room. Half-way down one side sat Miss Letty, leaning forward in her chair, an eager color in her gentle face. She expected to enjoy this so much. It was not often that Mammachen could be persuaded to go to the theatre, and here was the theatre come to them.

Slowly and somewhat heavily did the Phenix get under way, shaking his crest once or twice as if to free himself, but rising gallantly as he caught the gusts of that great scene; and then ascending, whirling in swift gyre upon gyre, he swept onward down the splendid storm of Schiller's passion; and the frail English girl, who was half German after all, followed him with dilating eyes of admiration. She had never seen Herr Jarlson look so handsome.

As he paused at the end of the scene, there was a great clapping of hands.

"Is Herr Jarlson really a good actor?" asked Mrs. Dettmar of the Countess.

"That is for you to judge. I think so. He plays these First Lover rôles well, do you see, because he has so much feeling, and because he is young," she added, shrewdly; "but his voice and his face fit him admirably for old men's parts. You should hear him play *Polonius.*"

"You don't mean to say that he can make a living on the stage?"

"There is no doubt of it. He has had good offers here, but prefers to make his début in some provincial theatre. He is no fool, my Phenix."

There was a fresh burst of applause from the other end of the room. Herr Jarlson was going on. "I will give you the fifth scene in that same act," he said gravely, "where *Don Carlos* makes his love declaration to the young *Queen.*"

Again there was the perfect silence, broken
by his husky, fervent voice. The passage was
perfectly familiar to most of those in the room,
but Miss Letty had never seen it acted. It
made her tremble a little at the outset; that
hapless love was such a terrible thing. And
the poor *Queen*, to be married to a graybeard
when all the while she really loved the graybeard's son ! To marry the wrong person and
find it out when too late—too late—it would be
horrible. She wondered if *Philip II.* was fat
and bald like—like a certain person ; and then
she was ashamed of herself, and frightened at
the way Herr Jarlson looked at her. He
was playing his part to her ; he was pleading
there as *Don Carlos* with her alone, and his
gray eyes flashed so that she could not look
away from them. Her heart beat hard. It
was so hot there in the dining-room, and
something choked her. Why could she not
look away from him? Her head swam ; she
grasped her poor soiled fan as tightly as she
could, to hold on to herself, to make sure
that it was herself and not the *Queen*. But
she was the *Queen ;* it was she herself who was
saying :

> *"Sie wagen es, zu hoffen,*
> *Wo Alles, Alles schon verloren ist?"*

and yet it was not *Don Carlos*, but Herr Jarlson, who cried, in passionate answer :

" *Ich gebe Nichts verloren als die Todten.*"

The room whirled around. The actor's figure was lost in a gray blur—she caught at her chair to save herself from falling.

But Herr Jarlson had stopped, and the uproarious plaudits and the clinking of glasses brought her to her senses. The Jewess leaned over and said : "You are a little faint, Miss Letty?"

"Oh, no," she answered, "not now."

"Come, Phenix," cried the Countess, "we have had enough tragedy. You must help me light the tree now." Herr Jarlson bowed obediently, and they disappeared behind the folding-doors. Miss Letty sat there, strangely ill at ease. She was thinking.

Mammachen, whose black eyes had been riveted upon her daughter and the Phenix, was thinking too. She was a far-sighted woman, and that was a very distant horizon upon which she could not see a cloud like a man's hand. But she was nervous. That letter about the Major had upset her, and she had to talk to somebody. Sitting next her was Stubbworth, blinking in the light, and awaiting fearfully the distribution of the gifts. He had inner visions of the Phenix lying out on the Hasenheide in the morning.

"Herr Jarlson is a capital actor, isn't he?" she remarked affably, in English.

"Indeed he is," said Stubbworth; "he is a man of fine feeling."

"Ah?"

"He is very good - hearted. I was ill yesterday, and he spent nearly all the afternoon showing me his collection of coins."

Stubbworth spoke with some agitation.

"Of coins? I shouldn't have supposed that he could afford to have a collection of coins."

"Why, yes," was the eager answer. "Herr Jarlson's father is only a country clergyman, but his grandfather is a great land-owner. He sent him to the university of Christiania, and then here; and if all goes well with Herr Jarlson, he will inherit a very neat property."

"Indeed!" exclaimed the widow. "I—I am somewhat surprised. But that is very fortunate—for him, I mean. You are quite sure, Mr. Stubbworth?"

"Quite," said he. But his voice was lost in the Christmas hymn that all the others were singing as the doors drew back. There blazed the noble tree, decked with colored candles and cheap gilt, and all the *pension* admired it immensely, laughing like children when the fir-needles caught fire or the candles burned crookedly, and most of them had no thought beyond the peace and good-will of that ever-blessed time. But Stubbworth and the Phenix scarcely looked at the Christmas - tree ; they eyed the Countess as she distributed the presents that lay piled upon a table. At last she reached it ; that little package upon whose reception a romantic Norseman had staked his happiness. Stubbworth himself handed it to Miss Letty ; it was a *Prachtband* in ugly cover of red and gold. Herr Jarlson's card slipped from the title-page. Miss Letty's fingers shook ; she did not glance at the title.

"Mammachen ! " she exclaimed, in a helpless whisper. " He has sent me a gift, and I am to be betrothed to-morrow. What shall I do ? "

Mrs. Dettmar took up the card deliberately. It was a very stylish card, and " Philopena " was pencilled faintly upon it. She opened the book ; it was a copy of " Proverbs of all Nations."

" Letty, my dear, it is a philopena. He is a very sensible young man. Of course you must go and thank him."

The Phenix was standing apart from the

others, and Miss Letty obeyed. "Herr Jarlson," she said, falteringly, "it was so kind— it was very good—" and then their eyes met. She stopped, but she did not turn away; a deep blush crimsoned her face, as she stood looking up at him. Nor did he speak at first. Then his English came to him.

"Mees Letty," he whispered, "*I at*——"

But someone touched his arm. It was Mammachen. "Herr Jarlson," she said, with the black eyes straight in his face, "it was very thoughtful of you to give that useful book to my daughter. We have tea served in our room every afternoon at four; may we not see you there soon? Come, Letty, my dear, it is time for us to go."

IV.

THE Phenix did not go out to the Hasenheide and put a bullet through his brains;
on the contrary he dragged Mr. Stubbworth
around to the Café Bauer to partake of a most
excellent late supper. But they did not talk
about Miss Letty; the conversation was mostly
upon philology and the forthcoming edition of
the Homilies.

The next day, at four, Jarlson presented
himself at the Widow Dettmar's room, sipped
his tea with counterfeited pleasure, and answered several shrewdly disguised interrogations
about himself. He was as favorably received
as any young man could have been, but alas!
Miss Letty, to her mother's chagrin, had gone
out with the Countess to admire the Christmas
display in the Passage; and had stood so long
before each shop window that even the Countess's impatience did not bring them back to
the *pension* before Herr Jarlson had finished
his call. Miss Letty's delay had been inten-
tional; she dreaded talking with the Norwegian

again so soon after that strange moment and that inexplicable, half-uttered English sentence of the night before. Her professed admiration for the toys in the Passage was a makeshift for her frightened little heart; but Mammachen had no suspicion of this, and reprimanded her for her lack of courtesy to such a promising young man as Herr Jarlson. The widow was tempted to go farther and expose the deception of which Major Vischer had been guilty, but she did not have quite the heart to tell Miss Letty all. Her explanation, the night before, that the Major had been called to Saxony for a week on military service, must do for the present. That fact of itself should have been hard enough for the Major's *fiancée* to bear, and yet Mammachen thought that Letty had listened to the news without any very deep sense of disappointment. Upon almost every other subject the widow was extraordinarily unimaginative, but as a mother, and a provident mother, she had a sort of faith that something would happen before the week was over to make clearer her duty toward her darling child.

Nevertheless the week went by uneventfully. Herr Jarlson dropped in again for tea, it was true, but again Miss Letty absented herself. Sylvester Evening came, and as she sat with the others in the *pension* dining-room, after the eight-o'clock supper was over, the widow was sorely troubled. The Major might arrive at any moment. To be sure, she had sent a note to his lodgings asking him to come, not that night, but the next morning, when she proposed to herself to see him alone and charge him to his face with having deceived her about the property; but in his eagerness he might drive directly from the station to the *pension*, and then there would be a delightful state of affairs.

On Sylvester Evening it had long been customary at the *pension* to pass the time as merrily as possible until the old year was nearly gone, and then to sally forth to enjoy the brief carnival enacted each year in the Berlin streets at midnight. But the Widow Dettmar was in no mood for the songs and speeches and toasts which recalled the gayety of the week before. She sat in a corner with Miss Letty, and trembled whenever the door opened lest she might behold the radiant countenance of Major Vischer. The hours seemed to her to crawl so slowly by; the merriment was only a forced echo of Christmas; at any moment—to-morrow at the latest—the Major would arrive, and Letty, thanks to her mother's consideration,

was still ignorant of his baseness and unac-
countably obstinate in avoiding Herr Jarlson.
It was provoking. Gloomily did Mrs. Dettmar
survey the Phenix as he rose in obedience to
the Countess's desire and acted *Polonius*. He
was a worthy young man, with fine prospects
professionally and otherwise, and yet his *Polonius*, admirable as the Countess pronounced it to
be, appeared to Mrs. Dettmar to lack some of
the fervor which had characterized his *Don
Carlos*. Miss Letty sat with her eyes in her lap
all the time he was reciting. It was enough to
discourage the stoutest maternal heart.

Eleven o'clock came, then half-past. The
Major did not arrive. At a quarter to twelve
the company broke up in little parties. The
Countess asked Mrs. Dettmar and Miss Letty,
Herr Jarlson and Mr. Stubbworth, to accompany
her. Miss Letty was very silent as she put on
her wraps. Her mother, arraying herself in a
fur cape and straw hat—for she had gone without a winter bonnet for the sake of adding
to Letty's trousseau—watched her nervously.
The old year was almost gone ; with the next
morning would come the broken engagement,
and then another campaign on the part of a
devoted mother who had already fought her
best.

"Mr. Stubbworth," said the Countess, as they descended the huge winding staircase, "you shall escort Miss Letty, and you may talk English. My Phenix must watch over the Frau Lieutenant and myself." Mrs. Dettmar's heart sank again.

Dorotheen Strasse was perfectly still, save for a few hurrying groups of people like themselves. There was no moon, but the night was fine, and warmer than the day had been. They turned down Charlotten Strasse, past the black shadow of the Hôtel de Rome, and crossed Unter den Linden diagonally. The wide street was empty, but almost every building was still lighted, notwithstanding the lateness of the hour, and as they reached the southern side, they could see special policemen stationed everywhere. Just as the Countess's little company, keeping close together, started down Friedrich Strasse, somewhere, high up in that tranquil midnight air, a deep bell struck—one—two—Hark! There was a rush and roar of many feet, a manifold cry of confused voices, and in an instant hundreds and thousands of people poured into the narrow street, a black stream issuing from every building and alley-way, and on every lip there was the one jubilant shout :

"*Prosit Neujahr! Prosit! Prosit Neujahr!*"

"*Prosit!*" answered the Countess, as a workman shouted his greeting in her face, for the etiquette of this carnival demanded a perfect democracy of well - wishing. "*Prosit Neujahr!*" shrieked Herr Jarlson into the ear of a policeman, who was struggling to keep the crowd from trampling upon one another.

"*Prosit Neujahr!*" called out Miss Letty, vaguely, fearing a condign punishment from some source if she did not conform to the law of the hour; and back and forth surged the tumult, and higher and higher rose the boisterous greeting to the opening year.

Herr Jarlson was in front, trying to keep the ladies from being too roughly jostled, and at the same time to guard his silk hat, which he had foolishly worn, and which was considered a fair target for friendly blows. Suddenly he stopped. A large café had flung open its doors, and hundreds of men were pouring out across the pavement; it was impossible to force a passage for the moment, and the five people from the *pension* were crowded out toward the street by the pressure from behind. The dazzling electric light from the café streamed across the disorderly mass of figures in a wide bar as bright as day ; it gleamed on the faces of the men and women upon the opposite pavement.

" Oh, what is the matter over there ? " cried Miss Letty.

It was only a couple of shop-girls, without escort, teased by a ring of men. The same instant that Miss Letty spoke, a short man with sweeping mustache grasped one of the girls from behind and kissed her, then let her go again, and stood there with his face full in that brilliant bar of light, laughing at his New Year's joke. It was Major Vischer, in civilian's dress. Stubbworth recognized him, and instinctively threw himself in front of Miss Letty, that she might not have the shame of seeing who it was. But he was too late.

" Mammachen," said Miss Letty, in a choking voice, "can we not go home now? I am so tired ! "

" Why, yes, Letty," answered Mrs. Dettmar, who had been peering with some interest into the open door of the café ; " certainly, if you have seen enough ; " and with great difficulty they all turned around and began to struggle back through the on-coming crowd. The gentlemen made heroic efforts to clear a passage, but they were all separated more than once, and when they finally emerged into Unter den Linden again, Miss Letty was leaning against Jarlson's arm, Stubbworth was supporting the Countess, and Mammachen toiled painfully in the rear.   Then Stubbworth offered her his other arm, and she took it, her maternal heart beating fast as she saw Letty's slender figure close against the Norwegian's pelisse. Mrs. Dettmar knew very well that it was not conventional in Berlin to allow two young people to walk together like that; but then, did not Napoleon win his battles by ignoring the Prussian rules?

The Phenix and Miss Letty walked together, therefore, across Unter den Linden and up the silent Charlotten Strasse.   They walked slowly, the wide night above them, the uproar of the carnival growing fainter behind them, and before them was the New Year.   They said little. The obligation to which Miss Letty had struggled for a whole week to be faithful had been suddenly, and by no act of hers, destroyed.   She was certain that the Major could not have loved her, any of the time; but her chagrin was already lost.   It seemed hours since that moment back in Friedrich Strasse; that was at the Old Year's end, and now she was living in the New, as she and Herr Jarlson passed slowly, quietly toward home.

As they reached the *pension*, the others were close behind. Herr Jarlson unlocked the door, Miss Letty passed in, and he followed her. The Countess's foot was already on the lower step, when Mrs. Dettmar stopped.

"Wait," she said, "let us see if we can't still hear that shouting."

The three listened. Stubbworth thought he could detect a distant murmur; the Countess declared she could hear nothing at all; Mrs. Dettmar seemed to be in doubt.

"Wait," she insisted, "let us listen once more." But this time, after a longer trial, they all agreed that the noise had died quite away.

Miss Letty and the Phenix were awaiting them on the landing. Mammachen's sudden curiosity about the shouting had given these two a minute's time together. A minute is not much, but it is long enough for a simple English sentence.

When Mrs. Dettmar and her daughter were alone in their room, the girl broke down.

"I cannot marry Major Vischer," she sobbed, hiding her face upon her mother's robust bosom. "I do not love him. I cannot love him."

"Don't cry, Letty, my dear," said the widow, gently stroking her daughter's hot cheek, "don't cry—don't cry. If that's the way you feel about him, Mammachen will arrange it—Mammachen will arrange it."

. . . .

Mammachen arranged it. Two years later, when Dr. Stubbworth visited Berlin to get material for a new edition of the Homilies, the Countess told him on the night of his arrival that his old friend Herr Jarlson was playing Second Old Man with great success at the Deutsches Theatre, and that he might be seen sitting by the side of Mammachen almost any Sunday in the English chapel, gravely reading the responses. The next morning Stubbworth took an early stroll in the Thiergarten, and whom should he meet coming down the Sieges Allée but the Phenix, pushing a baby carriage with one hand, and with a play of Shakespeare in the other!

The Commonest Possible Story

THE COMMONEST POSSIBLE
STORY

PHILANDER ATKINSON, bachelor of
law and writer of light verse, sat one
murky August evening in his hall-bedroom,
with the gas turned low, wondering whether
the night would be too hot for sleep. At a
quarter before ten a loitering messenger-boy
brought him a line from his friend Darnel :
*Come around at once. Just back. The very
greatest news.* Thereupon Atkinson discarded
his smoking-jacket, reluctantly exchanged his
slippers for shoes, and took the car down to
Twelfth Street, remembering meanwhile that
Darnel's brief vacation from the Broadway
Bank expired that day, and speculating as to
the nature of the great news which the clerk
had brought back from Vermont. The lawyer
was a Vermonter, too, and it was this fact, as
well as a common literary ambition, that had
drawn the young fellows together at first, long
before Philander, on the strength of having two

triolets paid for, had moved up to Thirty-first Street. Philander Atkinson liked Darnel, admired his feverish energy and his pluck, envied his acquaintance with books. He had always persisted in thinking that Darnel's stories would sell, if only some magazine would print one for a starter; and he had patiently listened to most of these stories, and to some of them several times over. Yet Darnel had never had any luck; had never had even his deserts; and the sincerity of his congratulations whenever Atkinson's verses saw the light always caused Philander to feel a trifle awkward. He knew that the indefatigable clerk had two or three manuscripts " out "—out in the mails —when the vacation began, and as he turned in at Darnel's boarding-house he had almost persuaded himself that *The Æon* had accepted " Laki," his friend's Egyptian story. It was a long climb up to Darnel's room, and the writer of light verse mounted deliberately, being fat with overmuch sitting in his office chair. On the third floor the air was heavy with orange-flowers and Bonsilene roses, and a caterer was carrying away ice-boxes. A whimsical rhyme came into Philander's head, and he made a mental note of it. Just then Darnel appeared, leaning over the balustrade of the fourth - floor landing, his coat off, his collar visibly the worse for the railway journey, and an eager smile upon his thin, homely face.

"Hullo, D.," said Philander. "Here I am. Been having a wedding here?" he added in a low voice, as he grasped Darnel's hand.

"I believe so. I'm just back. Come in, Phil. You got my message?"

"Why else should I be here, old fellow? Is it 'Laki,' sure?"

Without answering, Darnel led the way into his tiny room. His trunk lay upon the floor, half unpacked, the folding-bed was down, for the better accommodation of some of the trunk's contents, and the desk in the corner, under the single jet of gas, was covered with piles of finely torn paper. Darnel's manner, usually nervous and somewhat conscious, betrayed a certain exhilaration, but he was under perfect self-control.

"'Laki?'" he said, seating himself in his revolving chair and whirling around to the desk, while Atkinson threw himself upon the bed, "'Laki?' Oh, I had forgotten. It's probably here." He pulled over the mail accumulated during his absence. "Yes." He tore open the big envelope. "'The editor of *The Æon* regrets to say,' etc.;" and he tossed the printed slip, with the manuscript, into his waste-basket, with a laugh.

Atkinson's heart sank. Poor Darnel; it was not a cheerful welcome home. But Darnel was busied with his letters.

"And here are the others," he went on. "I thank the Lord none of them were accepted."

"What!" exclaimed Philander, turning upon his elbow.

Darnel looked at him with a puzzling smile.

"That's why I sent for you," said he. "Phil, all that I've been writing here for three years is stuff, and I've only just found it out. I can do something different now."

Atkinson stared. Darnel had rarely talked about his own work, and then in a scarcely suppressed fever of excitement and anxiety. Many a time had Atkinson noticed his big, hollow eyes turn darker, and his sallow face grow ashy, even in reading over with a shaking voice some of that same "stuff."

"I have learned the great secret," Darnel added, quietly.

"You have Aladdin's ring?" said Atkinson. "Or are you in love?"

"Both," replied Darnel. "It is the same thing."

Philander flung himself back upon the pillow, with a little laugh. "Go ahead, D."

"I have found her, and myself. Let me turn down the gas a little; I see it hurts your eyes. I belong in the world now; I am in the heart of it—I said to myself coming down the river this afternoon—in the heart of the world." He lingered over the words. "Phil," he exclaimed, suddenly, "all the time I was trying to write I was really trying to lift myself by the boot-straps. I was laboring to imagine things and people, and to get them on paper. It was all wrong. Do you remember that French poem you read me last winter, about the idol and the Eastern princess—how she lay on her couch sleeping—the night was hot—with the bronze idol gazing at her with its porphyry eyes, while her brown bosom rose and sank in her sleep, and the porphyry eyes kept staring at her—staring—but they never saw? Well, I believe my eyes have been like that. In 'Laki,' now, you know I wanted to describe the exact color of the stone in the quarry, and asked the Egyptologist up at the Museum to tell me what it was? He laughed at me. Very well. It was a dull-red stone, with bright-red streaks across it; I saw the same thing in Troy this afternoon, when a hod-

carrier fell five stories and they picked him up
from a pile of bricks.''

'' You're getting rather realistic,'' muttered
Philander.   Darnel was not looking at him,
and went on unheeding.

'' I have but to tell what I see.   I have
stopped imagining ; my head has ached—Phil,
you don't know how it has ached—trying to
imagine things.   I am past that now ; if you
only shut your eyes and look, it is all easy.
Take that old Edda story that I tried to work
up, about the fellow who fought all day long
against his bride's father, and when night came
the bride stole out and raised all the dead men
on both sides, by magic, so that the next day,
and every day, the battle raged on as before.
I used to plan about the magic she used, and
tried to invent a charm.   Why, all she did
was to pass over the battle-field at night, where
the dead lay twisted in the frost, and while the
wolves snarled around her and the spray from
the fiord wet her cheek, she stooped to touch
the dead men's wrists ; and they loosed their
grip upon broken sword and split linden shield,
their breath came again, soft and low like a
baby's, and so they slept till the red dawn.''

'' Look here,'' said Atkinson, sitting up very
straight, '' you've been reading ' The Finest

Story in the World,' and it has turned your head."

" Oh, the London clerk who was conscious of pre-existences, and forgot them all when he fell in love? I could have told Rudyard Kipling better than that myself." Darnel gave an impatient whirl to the revolving chair.

" You mean you think you can," replied Atkinson, sharply.

" As you like." He spoke dreamily, and Atkinson dropped back on the pillow again, watching his friend as narrowly as the dim light would allow. Hard work and unearthly hours had told on Darnel; he certainly seemed light-headed.

" Sickening heat — black frost — " he was murmuring; " marching, stealing, fighting, toiling—joy, pain—the life of the race—is a man to grow unconscious of these things in the moment that he really enters the life of the race, that he feels himself a part of it? What do you think, Phil?"

" I think," was the slow reply, " that whatever has happened to you in Vermont has shaken you up pretty well, old fellow. They say that when someone asked Rachel how she could play *Phèdre* so devilishly well, she just opened her black Jewish eyes and said, ' I have seen her.' And I think, in the mood you're in now, you can see as far back as Rachel or anybody else. It's like being opium-drunk ; if you could keep so, and put on paper what you see, you could beat Kipling and all the rest of them. But you can't keep drunk, and you can't write prose or verse on love-delirium. It's been tried.''

'' Suppose Rachel had said, ' I *am Phèdre ?* ' ''

Atkinson lifted his stout shoulders, laughing uneasily. '' So much the worse. I should say, the less pre-existence of that sort the better. You might as well tell me the whole story, D. What is her name ? ''

'' In a moment. She loves me, Phil. She is waiting for me in her little house among the hills. I left her only this morning, and soon I shall go back and leave New York forever. I can write the story up there—the story I have dreamed of writing—for I shall always have the secret of it. I have but to shut my eyes and tell what I see ; and it is because she loves me. All the life of all the past — I can call that ' A Story of the Road.' Then there will be the future to write of—the men and women that are to come ; for we shall have children, Phil, and in them——''

"You're making rapid progress," ejaculated Philander.

"——I shall know the story of the future. Even now I know it; I do not simply foresee it, I see it. Why not 'A Story of the Goal!' For I belong to it—do you not understand? Yet, after all, what is that compared with the present? It shall be 'A Story of the March!' Look there!"

He threw his eyes up to the ceiling, which was brightened for an instant by the headlight of an elevated train as it rushed past.

"Do you know what that engineer was really thinking of as he went by? That would be story enough. Or what was in the heart of the bride to-night, down on the third landing — you smelled the orange-flowers as you came up? To feel that your heart is in them, and theirs in you——"

But Philander Atkinson was not listening to the lover's rhapsody. He was thinking of a certain summer when he, too, had had strange fancies in his head; when his thoughts played backward and forward with swift certainty; when he had grown suddenly conscious of great desires and deep affinities, and for a space of some three months he had dreamed of being something more than a mere verse - maker, a master of the file. Then—whether it was that she grew tired of him, or they both realized that some dull mistake had been made — it was all over. There was still in his drawer a package of manuscript he had written that summer : in blank verse, none too noble a form for the high thoughts which then filled him ; in a queer new rhythm, too, the secret of whose beat he had caught at and then lost, for the lines read harshly to him now. He looked these things over occasionally, as a sort of awful example of himself to himself ; though he had gone so far as to borrow some of their imagery, not without a certain shame, to adorn his light verse. His card-house had fallen, but some of the colored pasteboard was pretty enough to be used again. Curiously, he found that he could cut pasteboard into more ingenious shapes than ever since his brief experience in piling it ; fancy served him better after imagination left him ; his triolets were admirably turned, and his luck with the magazines began. Altogether it had been an odd experience ; half those crazy ideas of Darnel had been his two years before, but he was quite over them—yes, quite —and now it was D.'s turn. He listened again to something that Darnel was murmuring.

" And she is an ordinary woman, one would

say ; a common woman.   That is the mystery
and the glory of it.   I do not know that she is
even beautiful.   There must be thousands of
women like her ; I can see it plainly enough,
that there must be thousands of women in the
world like *her.*"   There was a reverent hush in
his voice.

Atkinson choked back an exclamation. Was
Dr.'s head really turned ? " A common woman"
—" not know whether she is beautiful ? "   A
face rose before him, unlike any face in all the
world : eyes with the blue of Ascutney, when
you look at it through ten miles of autumn
haze ; hair brown as the chestnut leaf in late
October ; mouth——

Philander trembled slightly, and rising to his
feet, stood looking down at Darnel, haggardly.
It was quite over, that experience of two sum-
mers before, but while it lasted he had at least
never dreamed that there were thousands of
women in the world like *her.*

" Sit down, Phil, I am almost through.   A
woman like other women, and the story, when
I write it, a common story.   It will be the
commonest possible story ; common as a rose,
common as a child.   I am going back to Vermont, where I was born, and where I have
been born anew.   There will be plenty of time

for the story—years, and years, and years. I have only to close my eyes some day, and she will write down all I tell her, and I shall call the story hers and mine."

But Atkinson still stood, his hands in his pockets, his heavy figure stooping, the lines hardening in his face, while he watched the rapt gaze of Darnel, and drearily reflected how strange it was that a woman should open all the gates of the wonder-world to one man's imagination, and that some other woman should close those secret gates, quietly, inexorably, upon that man's friend.

"Wait," said Darnel. "Must you go back to your triolets? Let me show you her picture first." He turned the gas up to its fullest height, and held out a photograph.

It was the same woman.

An Incorrigible Poet

AN INCORRIGIBLE POET

IT was the very end of summer, and there were yellowing leaves upon the lower branches of the birches that lined a narrow valley in the Vosges. But not a leaf was stirring in the dead air of the late forenoon, and Philander Atkinson, American poet, climbed slowly and with some weariness along the bed of the shrunken stream. He was thinner than three years before, when he had had that strange talk with his friend Darnel, and had shortly after sailed for Europe without even bidding Darnel good-by. This last June the fever had clutched him at Capri. All through July and August he had lain in a hospital on the hill-slope above Naples, and it was only within two weeks that he had felt able to get North again, and to try a walking-trip, by easy stages, in lower Alsace. To-day he shifted his knapsack restlessly. The glare of the sun made him dizzy after a while and he wondered if he had quite thrown off the fever.

Just then the valley narrowed to a gorge; the birches and the sunlight fell away together, and the shadow of huge fir-trees blackened the creeping surface of a pool. At its head the streamlet slipped almost noiselessly over bright-beaded moss, at its foot the overflow trickled away again beneath an arch of heavy masonry, while right and left through the sombre firs stretched a Roman wall. Rome again! Atkinson threw off his knapsack and drank of the shadowed water, then lay back listlessly against the gray wall. Rome again!

There was no escaping her. Wherever he had wandered in Europe he had found the arch or the road, the word or law, that spoke still of the world's mistress. When he first landed he scarcely thought of the Mediterranean countries. A sudden legacy had set him free from the pretence of calling himself a lawyer, and he had taken passage for Germany with the duplicate proofs of his first volume of verses in his bag. To the second edition, issued the following autumn, he had added, " In Heine's Land," poems on German themes. For the Muses had been gracious to Philander, and keeping him far from the Germandom of lecture-rooms and barracks, had sent him into Thuringia and the Hartz, the Black Forest

and the Bavarian Alps, the last refuge-places of
Romance. Critical notices of " In Heine's
Land " which reached him from time to time
praised the advance upon the cleverness, the
mere brightness, of his earlier verse. His touch
was certainly softer, and now and then he
struck a deeper note than had been his wont
since he began to publish. In Bavaria he always went to church. An old priest who was
his companion for a week at a Salzburg inn
thought him ripe for conversion, and Atkinson
did indeed come to the conviction that some of
his walk and conversation with Darnel in New
York had been rather godless. A new world of
emotional life opened before him. He comprehended instinctively, as he thought, such
apparently separate phenomena as the South
German peasant, the early drawings of Dürer,
and the heart-breaking change of key in Heine's
songs. Back of the thirteenth century his
mind rarely wandered, nor very far forward into
the nineteenth, and he thought seriously of
renting a couple of rooms in Marburg Castle and
settling down to the new dream of his life, the
revivification of romantic poetry.

Then, one restless day, he promised a friend,
a young Australian painter, to spend the next
winter on the Nile. It was an evil hour for

Philander, and the guardian Muses must have slept. Little by little the North faded from his mind : its art, its serious faith, his own imaginative impulse—all these grew unreal under the Egyptian sky. But he never wrote such facile verse as on the deck of the dhahabîyeh, pipe in mouth, with the Australian forever interrupting him to discuss color-values. He discovered that three or four dozen Arabic words enlarged his rhyme - list marvellously, and that his readers liked that sort of thing. " Oriental Overtones," a collection that his publishers issued in the spring at a dollar and a quarter, the cover ornamented with a pink camel squatting before a blue pyramid, was lauded for its gorgeous imagery and sonorous diction, and netted poor Philander in the first six months the munificent sum of twenty-seven dollars and a half. Poor Philander — for the Australian told him that the " Overtones " were " rot," and he knew it well enough himself.

They parted in Syria, the American journeying westward, along a Roman road. But he lingered on the shores of the Mediterranean, for here he made new discoveries in himself. He found a sense of beauty impatient of mystery or awe, a feeling for the harmony of line, a satisfaction in subtleties of light and shade.

He gazed at blue water and volcanic headland and graying temple until he felt that his eye was right at last. An enthusiasm for the classics, forgotten since his school-days, awoke in him. There was no use in trying to write like Byron or even like Uhland, but he really thought, after two months in Sicily, that he could imitate Theocritus. At least he translated Theocritus, then turned to Virgil and Horace again, steadied his sense of form, trained himself into a cool paganism of temper, and wrote verses delicate yet firm in outline as the sculptures on a sarcophagus. Henceforward he determined to be a classicist, to restrict the quantity of his poetry, to be less lavish with its hues, less individual in its form, but to aim at perfection. He quite outgrew, as he supposed, that transient mediævalism. His dreams went backward to the lovely Græco-Roman world, and forward too, for one day, on the rocks at Capri, he saw more clearly than ever before what might, with good fortune, be his place among twentieth-century poets. And the next day the fever took him. Rome and Sicily, Marburg and the Nile, alternated with one another in his delirium for weeks and weeks, while the sisters of the hospital counted quiet prayers for him, pagan as he was.

It was of all this that Philander was thinking, as he lay there in the Alsatian valley, with his head against a Roman wall. The coolness of the place was infinitely restful, and the fir-forest brought back many an outworn dream. He watched the eddies of the pool circle away from a broad rock that lay mid-stream, its top almost touched by the stealthy water, and thought of the folk - lore of the North, the stories of Undine and of the water-sprites, the maidens of the spring and nymphs of the wave, and thence his mind wandered aimlessly to the sea-goddesses of the South. Scarcely could he keep his eyelids apart, so drowsy had he grown, and he smiled drowsily at his own fancies, and wished the fever had left his head steadier for these long mornings in the Alsatian sun.

.   .   .   .

All at once she was there—her feet just free from the clear ripples which washed that broad rock in the middle of the pool, the water still trickling from her glistening limbs and luminous body, and dripping from her upraised arms as she knotted her wet yellow hair. Then she leaned forward, with fingers clasped about her rounded knees, her friendly blue eyes fixed upon Philander, and a slight inscrutable smile upon the full contented lips.

" My brother "—she said, and he knew her at that word, and his breath came slower. It was no maiden of the spring, nor wave-born goddess of the doves ; she was the calm Classic Muse whose inspiration he had sought at many a lonely place and quiet hour on the shore of the Mediterranean.

" Shall I tell you something, my brother ? I have known you a long while, ever since that day at Brindisi, when you thought you turned your back forever on the North. I pitied you at Capri for your fruitless gazing across the water, and I wished to come to you in your fever, while the black-robed sisters were asleep. But it is better that I waited until now. Do you not know, poor boy, that it is all in vain that you seek me ? You were born too late, and I, who am very old—you need not smile— know very well that no hour comes twice, not even to us of the timeless world. There were two men in this century of yours who might perhaps have given themselves to me utterly. One was a Jew boy who fell in love with his cousin and broke his heart, so that I could not teach him a single note, though he and I sat to- gether one noon in the Hartz forest, and he used to cry out for me passionately now and then. The other was a tall Englishman whose heart was troubled about his God, so that he could look at me only for a moment, though I drew near him more than once in the high Alps. They were born too late, like you, and into a world which is not mine. But what matters it? Each to his own world. Why do you give yourself the fever? I love you, my brother of this strange new age, but you must never try to behold me any more. You have your own world, and I am told it is a brave one : why do you look back ? "

.   .   .   .

Atkinson opened his eyes slowly. The stream-let was still murmuring over the moss, but no voice mingled with its tune ; upon the broad rock a gray bird was tilting, and the beautiful nude form no longer gleamed against the brown shadows. He sprang to his feet. His head felt strangely clear. The dizziness had gone, as if the lingering Italian fever had been exorcised by his draught from the mountain stream, but a lassitude had taken its place. He knew he had been dreaming, yet he felt ten years older than when he had flung himself down against that lichen-covered wall. Something was broken in him. He remembered each syl-lable that had fallen from those musical, sensu-ous lips, and for an instant his own heart lay

open before him as the water - deeps. The
dream-divinity was right : no hour comes twice.
The hour for that fair Græco-Roman world was
past, and not even a poet could bring it back
again, or strive to tarry in it save to his own
hurt. How blind he had been, ever since that
day at Brindisi !

Mechanically he shouldered his knapsack,
and started up the valley. His feet stumbled
once and again upon the narrow path, and he
wondered if he had strength enough to finish
the climb to Ueber-See-und-Thal — a famous
monastery once, then a convent, but half secu-
larized now and become a show-place. The
rocky wall of the gorge kept crowding closer
upon the thin stream, sliding inertly from pool
to pool. The air was heavy with balsamic
odors ; at every turn in the path there was
something to remind Philander of that world of
romance which had so long held him captive.
It was like getting home again. Here was a
hollow under the cliffs fit for a *Siegfried's* drag-
on ; there a lonely rock-walled glade like the
one in the incantation scene of " Der Frei-
schütz." Airs of operas, bits of poetry, whimsical legends, slipped back into his mind as if
they had never been absent from it. As he
neared the valley's head there was a view back-

ward through the jagged fir-trees, past the sunlit
hazy slopes of birch and beech, and out upon
the wide Rhine-plain, misty even in high noon ;
and there was a charm, a mysterious fascination
about it all, after those clear, pale distances in
Italy !

But he was too weary to stand looking, and
pushed on across the hot pasture-land and up
to the walls of Ueber-See-und-Thal. The
path led him close to the door of the lower
chapel, and he loosened his knapsack and went
in. His guide-book had told him that the
chapel to Mary of the Fir-tree was very old, yet
he was scarcely prepared for the crudeness and
simplicity that marked the interior, as his eye
grew accustomed to its twilight. The sandstone statue of the Virgin belonged to the ear-
liest period of Northern sculpture ; the black
font was worn deeply at the side by centuries of
finger-touches ; the rude benches of darkened
pine were soiled with the candle-drippings of
Alsatian pilgrims. Faith was still unshaken in
this nook of the Vosges. Before the tawdry,
pitiful altar was crouching an old woman, her face
bowed to her knees, her crooked fingers trembling over her rosary ; and the huge stone pillar
by the door, built when Barbarossa was a child,
was hung around with votive offerings—poor

little tin figures of broken limbs, and waxen hearts, and yellowing slips of paper laboriously written with "Pray for Me," "Pray for Us," "Dear Mary of the Fir-tree, I am Thankful." Philander murmured the words softly to himself, before he went out.

A few sisters of the suppressed religious order had been allowed to remain at Ueber-See-und-Thal to provide for the wants of the pilgrims and sight-seers, and the American was shown to the refectory and served with a dinner of boiled beef and turnips, with black bread and the white wine of Oberhausbergen. The nun who waited upon him had a round, childish face, with eyes serious as a Madonna's and of a brown that he had never seen outside of the Black Forest. She spoke French badly. Philander watched her, and as he finished the simple meal, pointed to the open door of the refectory.

Far below was the Rhine, and beyond it, almost hidden in the haze, there were dim mountain lines.

"That is the Hornisgründe over there, is it not?" he asked, in the Black Forest dialect.

A startled look came into her eyes, and her grave mouth grew curiously wistful.

"Certainly," she answered, in the same drawling gutturals, without following the direc-

tion of his hand. " That is the Hornisgründe."
She paused a moment in embarrassment. " I
thought you were not French. The gentleman
is an American."

" But I have lived in the Black Forest," asserted Philander, " for months and months."

" And I was born there." She glanced
toward the doorway now, as if scarcely conscious of the stranger's presence.

" I was sure of it. And how came you
here ? "

He had gone too far. She turned to him,
almost with terror.

" No, no ! " she cried. " You must not ask.
I have been here a long time, and—I am very
happy."

Philander lifted his eyebrows. " Do you
mean that ? " he remarked, quietly.

For answer she looked away from him, and
gathered up the empty dishes without a word.

When she returned she brought his coffee,
and spoke French.

" Would Monsieur not prefer to take coffee
upon the terrace ? The view is very beautiful,
and people come a long distance to see it."

He rose and walked to the doorway, the nun
following with a sugar-bowl and a tiny flask of
chartreuse. The blazing sunlight made him

hesitate. He turned irresolutely, and took a long look at the cool, dim refectory, with its dark oak timbers and whitewashed walls, and at the Black Forest woman, with her calm eyes—and her mask of French — and her unknown history.

"Why do you look back?" she asked, naïvely.

Philander was strangely moved ; those were the very words spoken by the smiling goddess of his morning dream ; but could he not linger even in the shadow-land of Romance? He made no answer.

"There is a breeze under the linden by the north door," she went on, "and there are tables there. I will show you."

He followed, without noticing whither she was taking him. "There, Monsieur," she said, "here is the coffee, and the sugar, and the liqueur, and—" in a lower voice—"here are some Americans—adieu ! "

Philander raised his eyes. It was too late to retreat, and besides he recognized Virginia Johnson, a former table companion at the boarding-house on Twelfth Street. She was a student at the Art League then, on the eve of going to Paris. .

"Why, Mr. Atkinson ! " she cried, dropping

the illustrated paper she was perusing, and putting out her hand joyfully, "this is delightful."

"Thank you," said Atkinson, rescuing her paper from its dangerous proximity to her coffee-cup. "You still read *Life*, I see."

"Of course. 'While there's *Life*, there's hope.' Do you remember the triolet? Or have we forgotten our humble beginnings, sir?"

It seemed natural to have Virginia Johnson chaff him.

"No," he said, "I haven't forgotten. That triolet in *Life* was the first thing of mine to be accepted, and I have never doubted that it was your thumbnail sketch that made them take it. And—excuse me—wasn't that your first acceptance too? And the week it came out you got the number first and gave it to me at dinner, with 'While there's *Life*, there's hope' marked in red."

She bowed with mock gravity. "You deserve your fame, Mr. Atkinson. You are loyal to that dear old boarding-house. Let me introduce you to my father."

An elderly gentleman in gray, with a felt hat pushed well back upon his bald head, laid down his newspaper and set his eyeglasses higher upon his nose.

"This is Mr. Atkinson, papa—Mr. Philander Atkinson.'' She repeated the words impressively, as if hoping that her father would recognize a name already distinguished in the world of minor poetry. But Mr. Johnson shook hands in utter innocence of the honor conferred upon him, and was conscious only of the pleasure in meeting a fellow-citizen.

'' Glad to know you,'' he said. '' I tell you it seems good to find an American over here. Haven't seen one since we left Heidelberg; there were lots of 'em there. That was a week ago, wasn't it, Virginia? ''

'' Three days,'' replied the girl, smiling.

'' Well, it's long enough, anyhow. There are nice places here in Europe, Mr. Atkinson, but a man gets kind of lonesome, doesn't he? ''

'' Sometimes,'' admitted Atkinson, putting a lump of sugar into his coffee.

'' Exactly. I should say he did! My daughter, now, has been over here five years, and says she hasn't been homesick once. I don't understand it; '' and he shook his bald head dubiously.

'' Papa has been away from New Jersey exactly five weeks,'' commented Miss Johnson. '' We have made I don't know how many business calls on woollen manufacturers—what comical times we have had!—and now I want him to go to Normandy for a month—to see some of the places where I've sketched, you know—and he insists upon our taking the steamer next Saturday. Can't you talk to him, Mr. Atkinson?"

The man of woollens smiled imperturbably, and took out a couple of cigars. "I wish you'd try one of those," he said. "I brought over a couple of boxes; Virginia has been managing the custom-house end of it. And here's a *Sun*, if you like; we got our papers at Mühlhausen last night, and haven't had time to read 'em until now. Nine days from New York to Mühlhausen isn't so bad, eh?"

But Philander declined the newspaper. The talk drifted to Miss Virginia's art-studies in Paris, and by and by Mr. Johnson dropped out of it, and buried himself contentedly in the New York stock quotations. Atkinson found himself studying the girl curiously as she chatted on. Was she the little Miss Johnson of five years back, who used to come in from Newark for five days in the week, and spar with Darnel and himself at dinner-time? She must have been barely eighteen then, but had already learned to manage her gray eyes with absolute accuracy and irreproachable composure. She had been on fire for Art, but as to everything else cool as a woman of thirty. When Philander's triolet, illustrated with her sketch, had been accepted by *Life*, he had grown distinctly sentimental over their joint production, but she laughed him down to a prose level in no time, and pocketed her half of the eight dollars with a most professional air. There was no nonsense, Darnel had once remarked oracularly, about Virginia Johnson ; and when her father sent her to Paris, even the most acrimonious woman among the Twelfth Street boarders found nothing to criticise in her conduct, and could not help wishing her well.

And this, Atkinson reflected, as he watched the radiant creature opposite him, was little Miss Johnson ! She was grown taller now and more womanly in figure ; her hair was done up differently, as far as the Paris hat would allow him to observe, and instead of the faint, clear color that she had had that winter in New York, her face was full-blooded and sun-browned, for she had been painting in the open air since May. Her eyes only were unchanged, but even they seemed more brilliant than of old. For a poor fellow just escaped from the black-robed sisters of a hospital, Miss Johnson's travelling gown was a miracle of Parisian audacity. Its color reinforced 'her eyes' peculiar gray, and the long suède gloves that lay by the *Life* upon the little table were exactly the shade of her coiled hair. More marvellous still to the jaded spirits of Philander, was the pulse-beat of a strong personality beneath this feminine and sophisticated charm. Through the clearness of her gay voice there was the subtle thrill that comes only with the consciousness of success. He remembered now that his friend the Australian, when fresh from Paris, had told him about some medal or other that Virginia Johnson had won, and he wondered why he had not paid more attention at the time. But there was something more than medal-winning back of that unobtrusive faith in herself.

"And yet you are going back to New York?" he said rather discontentedly, as she finished an exposition of the latest impressionist fad.

"Of course," she replied. "I've already rented my studio. Why not?"

"Oh, I don't know. What's the use?" he asked, suddenly.

She looked grave. "Have you done anything since 'Oriental Overtones'?"

"You saw those?"

"Most certainly." She did not tell him that she had cut the verses from the American papers wherever she had found them, and had cherished them for old acquaintance' sake, though knowing perhaps better than anyone how bad they really were.

"Yes, I have done a good deal since then. But a very beautiful woman—and a person who ought to know, I suppose—intimated to me no longer ago than this morning that I have been tarrying among the tombs." His eyes were half-closed as he spoke, and he heard again the plash of water into the pool by the Roman wall. But there was a sort of mockery in his voice that Miss Johnson did not like.

"Where have you been this summer?" she asked, somewhat at random.

"Since June, up to two weeks ago, in a Naples hospital. It was not particularly cheerful. Before that I was at Capri, and Paestum, and Taormina."

"I did not know you had been ill!" exclaimed Miss Johnson. "Why did you not let——" She stopped, flushing a little. "Anyone of the Paris boys would have gone down. You ought to be ashamed of yourself! And there was nothing about it in the papers from home."

"No," he said, "such is fame!"

"But what lovely places you have seen," said the young woman, with a change of tone.

"Yes, if you don't take the fever," he replied quietly. "And if you don't try to raise the dead to life."

It occurred to Miss Johnson that the fever might not have altogether left Mr. Atkinson's brain. Involuntarily she glanced toward her father, who had strolled away to the edge of the terrace, and was trying to focus a field-glass upon the haze-hidden spire of the Strasburg cathedral.

"Did you happen to see 'In Heine's Land'?" asked Atkinson.

She nodded.

"I wish you would tell me what you thought of it. Really thought of it, I mean ; just as you did of the triolet before we sent it to *Life*."

She remembered, all too distinctly, the fun she had made of his triolet, but he was appealing now to her candor as well as her artistic sense.

"I thought there were beautiful things 'In Heine's Land,'" she said, hesitatingly ; "very gentle and very perfect in feeling. I was reminded of one of them this morning—may I say so ?—when we were in the lower chapel and I read to papa some of those prayers hung upon the pillar. Do you remember your own poem about one of those ill-spelled prayers ? Then you ought to, if you please ! And yet—you know you asked

me to say it, Mr. Atkinson—is it really the best
work you can do ? Isn't it too foreign, too
mediæval, somehow ? I know those old German
motifs are the loveliest things in the world,
almost ; they make me cry, and yet all the time
I can't help thinking that they are not for us.
Haven't we something better ? An artist simply
must not hark back—you should have heard our
boys in Normandy talk that to each other ! You
see one can't, if one wants to, and—you will
forgive me, won't you ?—wouldn't it be better
not to try ? "

She was leaning across the table.

" I daresay," he said, wearily, yet wondering
a little why she had cared enough for his work to
tell him the truth about it, and not quite free
from the masculine fondness for a pretty woman's
preaching ; " but if a man is going to accom-
plish anything, he must do the best he knows at
the time."

" Most certainly ! " she cried. " I don't
mean that it wasn't worth doing, then, if you
were in the mood. I never saw anything more
touching than those bits of paper in the chapel.
And I wanted immensely to sketch that nun who
waited on us at dinner. You see I make that
concession to Romance ! Yet I imagine the
poor creature, in spite of her face, is prosaic

enough at bottom. It's partly her robe, you know, and the half-light of the refectory."

"Perhaps," said Philander, "but you should have seen her eyes fill when I spoke to her in German. She comes from over there"—he nodded toward the Rhine—"and she has a history, or she never would have left the Schwarzwald for the Vosges."

Miss Johnson was silent.

"It's a little thing like that," he went on, impetuously, with a subdued passion in his voice, "that makes me imagine there is still a place for poetry in the world. Here and there is an unspoiled corner of it, like Ueber-See-und-Thal, but there are not many of them left. Did you know there was a railway tunnel beneath the rock where the Lorelei used to sing?"

"No," she answered, slowly, "but do you not suppose, Sir Poet, that you could find women reclining in those railway carriages who are all the Lorelei was, and more?"

"You are talking like Archie Darnel now," said Atkinson, dryly, but his heart beat quicker in spite of himself.

"Yes? Tell me about Mr. Darnel. He used to be so ambitious, and I have never heard from him."

"Did you not know? Darnel and his wife

were killed on their wedding journey, three years ago."

"How terrible!" she murmured. "And how strange, after all Darnel meant to do!"

"There was nothing so very strange about it," remarked Philander, bitterly; "it was the most commonplace accident in the world. A drunken brakeman forgot to flag a train, and so spoiled the great story."

"What story? I don't understand."

"Well," said Atkinson, "I didn't altogether understand myself, but Darnel's idea was this—" and he told of the ecstasy of his friend concerning the Commonest Story. But he failed to mention the fact that he too had known Mrs. Darnel, and that he had sailed for Europe the day before the wedding. She listened gravely, but with a light kindling in her eyes.

"Ah!" she cried, as Philander finished, "if he had only lived! He was on the right track, was he not? If anything great is ever again to be done, it will be in that way. Darnel is on my side—or rather on our side—there are so many of us! There are pictures, poems, operas —oh, there are a thousand things to be done, and we *fin-de-siècle* people, we science-spoiled people"—there was a fine irony in her tone— "must do them. And we shall do them! It is grand to go back to New York. Just think of the men and women there all trying for the same thing, and all trained for it, too ! And the great story may be written any day, or the great picture painted. Oh, it is beautiful here in your quiet corner of Ueber-See-und-Thal, and it was beautiful in Normandy, but it always makes me restless to get to Paris or London or New York. Work—*work*—don't you fairly thrill with the sound of the word ? *'Men my brothers, men the workers '*— Please, Mr. Poet, what is the rest of it ? "

Philander shook his head. He was watching her as a sick man watches for the daybreak. The artist in her was all on fire—but the woman ? New thoughts, or rather old, forgotten thoughts, surged up within him. He took the chance.

" Yes," he said, deliberately, " you talk exactly like Archie Darnel. But Darnel was in love—body and soul in love."

Their eyes met. Virginia Johnson's fell first, but in that single instant he was clairvoyant enough to perceive why she had illustrated his triolet, so long ago, and why she had been annoyed that he did not telegraph when he lay ill with the fever. She had cared for him all the time.

"Halloo, Mr.—— Mr. Atkinson!" called Miss Johnson's patient father from the terrace. "I wish you'd give me the exact direction of Strasburg. I can't tell whether I'm focused on that spire or not." Philander rose without a word and joined him, leaving Miss Virginia playing with her suède gloves. The Black Forest woman, who had been standing in the shadow of the refectory for several minutes, came forward to remove the coffee-cups. With a sudden impulse, the girl took out a gold piece, and thrust it into the nun's cool palm.

"Oh, no!" said she. "I must not."

"For the poor, then."

"If Mademoiselle desires. May you have the blessing of Our Lady of the Fir-tree!" Then she glanced toward Atkinson with a singular expression, and added, timidly: "And I wish you happiness, Mademoiselle."

"Hush!" replied Virginia, severely. But her heart was dancing.

"Where do you go from here?" inquired Mr. Johnson of Philander, when the location of the cathedral spire was definitely determined.

"I am going back to New York," said Atkinson. There was a ring in his own voice that surprised him.

"You don't say!" cried the elder man, delightedly. "Passage taken?"

"Not yet."

"Well, why not sail with me Saturday? It's the French line, and I'm afraid there won't be many Americans on board. You'd better join us."

"There will be Americans enough," said Philander, as they strolled back toward the linden. "But I don't know whether I may join you. That depends."

The Alsatian coachman whom Mr. Johnson had hired was fussing impatiently with his horses, for it was mid-afternoon. Philander stooped for his knapsack.

"You walked up all the way?" asked Mr. Johnson. "Ride down with us." Philander glanced involuntarily at Miss Virginia.

"You had better," said the girl, quietly. "He has been ill, papa," and in spite of her swiftness in reaching for the field-glass and turning away for a last look at the view, Atkinson saw the color mount into her face.

"That settles it," cried the woollen manufacturer, cheerily.

"Very well," said Atkinson, with a look that his hospitable fellow-countryman could not fathom. "We will let that settle it. And I

think I shall sail on La Champagne." His
heart was like a boy's.

"Coachman — put—in — that—knapsack."
The Alsatian obeyed. "See?" added Mr.
Johnson, triumphantly, turning to Philander,
"these fellows understand you if you only talk
plain United States to them. All the same, it
makes me lonesome to travel where there aren't
any Americans. I tell you, it doesn't do man
or woman any good to knock around too much
alone. That's just what I say to my daughter.
Isn't that so, Virginia?"

But Virginia, with field-glass directed rather
vaguely out upon the Rhine-plain, stood motion-
less, as if she had not heard ; whereupon Philander caught her travel-stained *Life* from the
table, swiftly folded it and thrust it into his inside pocket. He was an incorrigible poet, after
all.

Number Three

NUMBER THREE

*" It is very desirable that a missionary should be mar-
ried. . . . Nor is it well to defer all attention to the
subject till the eve of departure from the country, though
excellent wives have been obtained even then."—Manual
for Missionary Candidates, Revised Edition, Boston, 1891.*

THE suppers at Mrs. Jackson's boarding-
house were generally considered her most
successful effort of the day. There was an un-
deniable sameness about the breakfasts, and the
theological students who boarded there were
inclined to swallow their coffee morosely and
hurry to the seminary. The dinners might well
have been worse than they were, though meat
was always poor and high in Hartwell, and it
was impossible to keep a theologue very plump
at three dollars and a half a week. But by tea-
time Mrs. Jackson was wont to repent of her
small economies, and being a master-hand at
hashes and croquettes and hot pastry, she gained
for her suppers a reputation that spread through
the seminary. Then, too, her theologues, at
the close of the day, were usually in a cheerful

mood, and ready to be pleased with trifles, cul-
inary and otherwise. They saved their best
jokes, culled from the funny corner of the religious papers, for this evening meal. Here they
mimicked the professors, and delivered themselves oracularly concerning politics and science. Most of them were second- and third-
year men, and could chaff one another upon
preaching experiences, the size of congregations,
and the probability of calls. When all other
topics failed, there was one which had for them
a perennial fascination. Whether they ap-
proached it coyly, or with practised noncha-
lance, there was not a man out of the dozen
who did not feel that his future profession and
his past experience warranted him in mention-
ing woman with the assurance of one who knew
whereof he spoke. Matrimony was for them
no speculative and problematical affair, to be
meditated upon at idle moments as one of the
possibilities of a distant future ; very far from
it. Within two or three years at most, they
all expected to be married, as a matter of
course. Their widest usefulness in their chosen
calling—for instance—depended largely upon
the abnegation of the single state. Some of
them had been engaged to be married for years
and years ; there were faithful school-teachers

and farmers' daughters patiently waiting until their lovers should finish the college and seminary course. It happened, however, that most of Mrs. Jackson's boarders, though cherishing a blessed certainty as to their ultimate condition, were still open to conviction as to the exact person whom Providence might indicate as their life-companion; and this slight air of uncertainty as to particulars mingled curiously with their innocent cock-sureness about woman in general.

An outsider would have been more amused than irritated by it all, but there was only one non-theological boarder at the table, a nephew of Mrs. Jackson, who did chores for his board and attended the academy, and who was not old enough to sink his irritation in his amusement. Dan Jackson was wont to declare to his school-boy friends, that the nudges and winks and sly allusions to the ladies on the part of his aunt's boarders made him tired. Toward the spring of the year, when the mud began to dry up in the long street of Hartwell, and the elm-tree buds to redden, and the theologues to prepare for their final examinations, Dan Jackson's weariness perceptibly increased. Three of the graduates were to be married in a month, and each day they had to face a concealed battery

of comment and interrogation and conjecture
from their fellow-boarders. Then, too, there
was Leffingwell's case. Leffingwell was considered the best all-round man in the Senior
Class: a stubby, old-faced fellow from the Far
West, with a preternaturally wide skull—flat on
top—and with high cheek bones. His hair
was thin, and his big ears moved slightly as he
ate. Whenever he stated a proposition or in-
dulged in repartee, he closed his eyes, in order
to concentrate his faculties upon the question in
hand. He was entitled by rights to the Berlin
fellowship for the next two years, but in pur-
suance of a long-cherished wish, was about to
sail as a missionary to Senegambia. He had
refused two chairs of philosophy in Western
institutions, and was popularly reputed at the
seminary to have devised a philosophical system
of his own, completely reconciling the claims
of religion and of science. It was currently believed that as soon as he had mastered the Sene-
gambian tongue, he would publish his system
in that language in an abridged form, thereby
at once allaying the native philosophic doubt of
the Senegambians and putting them in touch
with the most recent Occidental thought. The
Board had already accepted him, provisionally.
His statement of faith was considered the most

masterly document composed by a Hartwell
man for ten years ; transparently simple in
outline, and Scriptural in terminology, but in-
wardly packed so full of Leffingwell's irrefrag-
able system that any attempt to pick flaws in it
was logically as dangerous as to meddle with
dynamite.   No serious criticism had even been
offered upon it, and there was but one obstacle
to Leffingwell's immediate embarkment for his
field.   He was a bachelor, and the Board preferred that its representative in Senegambia
should be a married man.

Leffingwell's plight was thoroughly appre-
ciated by his fellow-students, and three times a
day he was obliged to run the gauntlet of their
suggestions and admonitions.   Open raillery
was ventured upon but seldom, for Leffingwell's
deliberate way of closing his eyes and selecting
the adequate epithet for retort was disconcert-
ing to his adversaries.   Some of their choicest
witticisms, therefore, were reserved until after
Leffingwell's departure from the table.   One
evening late in April he was so manifestly
absorbed and ill-tempered, that two of the
theologues winked at each other as he left the
room.

" Leffingwell's rather down on his luck, isn't
he ? " remarked one.

" Looks like it. Can't say that I blame him, though : two refusals in three weeks must ruffle even a philosopher, eh ? How is that, Tommy ? "

" Speak for yourself, man. I don't know the sensation." And the youth glanced blandly at an engagement ring that he had worn for six years.

" How do you know he has had the mitten twice ? " put in another.

" Never mind that : it's straight. I've seen both their photographs. One of them preferred Japan, and the other didn't fancy him because he proposed by letter."

" Good for her," said the man with the ring. " He deserves to be blue."

" But that isn't the reason why he's blue now, Tommy," cried the other, delightedly. " Look here, you fellows won't say anything ? " There were but four or five boarders remaining at the table, and they all glanced up, except Dan Jackson, who was devouring one of his aunt's best hashes, with his eyes fixed, as always, upon his plate.

" Don't let it out," continued the well-informed young man, " but there's a No. 3 ! "

" No ! " " You don't say ! " " Come ! " were the incredulous ejaculations of Leffing-

well's associates.   They had not believed him
capable of such rapid manœuvring.

" Fact, though.   That fellow has an address-
book compiled by his aunt, and this girl was
third in the list.   She isn't as strong as No. 1,
nor as well educated as No. 2, but she is pretty,
and she has seven or eight thousand dollars in
her own right."

This array of facts was respectfully listened to
by all except Dan Jackson, who reached scorn-
fully across the table for some sweet pickles.
Dan was fifteen, and had a due contempt for
matrimonial gossip.

The speaker looked around the circle triumphantly before adding his remaining bit of
information.   " He's waiting her answer now
—and she's a Hartwell young lady."

There was a chorus of quick guesses and offers
to bet—no stakes—on naming her in three
chances ; but the well-informed youth rose, and
shoved his chair under the table.

" No," he said, uprightly.   " I've gone too
far now.   You don't get her name out of me."
As a matter of fact, though all he had said was
true enough, he did not know her name himself.   The others crowded after him out of the
room, with even more than the usual hilarity,
leaving young Jackson alone at the table.

Dan poured himself a final glass of milk, awaiting his aunt's entrance. He raised the milk to his lips, and then set it down again, with a troubled expression upon his freckled, homely face. He was trying to put two things together.

It had been his turn, on the previous Sunday evening, to take tea with his Sunday-school teacher, Miss Achsah Millicent. She had given him good things to eat, and had been very entertaining—she was the only nice Sunday-school teacher in Hartwell, as all the boys admitted—but when he had proposed going home, soon after tea, under the supposition that it was proper to mention going and then yield to persuasions to remain, she had not urged him to stay; and he had been forced to come away, in some chagrin. At the gate he had met this Leffingwell going in! He thought nothing of it at the time : theologues were always calling at Deacon Millicent's. But what he had just heard startled him. Suppose Leffingwell were really going to marry Miss Achsah?

By George, he, Dan Jackson, wouldn't allow it! She was too good for him ; a million times too good. She was the prettiest girl in Hartwell, if she was getting a little old, and the nicest girl anywhere. She ought to marry a big lawyer, or a hotel-keeper, or the president of a railroad. To think of her marrying a missionary, who had to get a wife or lose his job !

And she might be giving Leffingwell her answer that very minute. Dan gulped off his milk fiercely ; there was no time to lose. Something had to be done about it, and there was apparently no one but himself who would or could do anything. For a minute he gazed despairingly about the room ; then he looked suddenly at his cuffs and felt of his necktie. Mrs. Jackson came in.

"Dan'l," said she, "don't you think you better be a clearing off those dishes ?"

Dan rose with dignity. "I suppose you'll have to excuse me to-night, Auntie. I've got to make a call, right away."

"Why, Dan'l, where on earth are you going to make a call ?"

"On my Sunday-school teacher," said Dan, virtuously, and Mrs. Jackson mentally decided, for the second time that day, that after all was said about his breaking dishes, Dan'l's heart was in the right place, anyhow.

In a quarter of an hour the boy had arrayed himself in his Sunday suit, donned a red necktie and high collar, and had painfully written " D.

Webster Jackson '' in violet ink upon a bevel-
edged card. Then he started stiffly down the
long street toward Deacon Millicent's, his boyish
heart still full of stern suspicion and righteous
wrath.

Miss Achsah Millicent sat under the hanging-
lamp in the sitting-room, gazing abstractedly at
a map of Senegambia. She had on her best
cashmere; it was two years old, to be sure, but
she had put in full sleeves that spring, and had
added velvet cuffs. Perhaps it would last
until—well, until she had several new gowns at
once; then she wondered if they wore leg-of-
mutton sleeves in Senegambia; and then she
knew she was blushing, and she glanced timidly
around the immaculate room. She was all alone
in the house. The Deacon was attending a
conference meeting in an adjoining town. Her
mother had been dead for many years. Both
mother and father had early consecrated their
daughter to the service of the Lord in the foreign
field, if the way should be providentially opened.
The Deacon had told about it in prayer-meeting
so often that it was a standing joke in Hartwell
society; and the girl felt her heart beat faster
whenever her father rose to speak, through fear
that he might forget his promise and tell the
church again about that early vow. For thus

far there had never been providentially opened a way to its fulfilment.

Achsah Millicent had known many theological students who expected to be missionaries, and some of them had been very good friends of hers, but none of them had ever asked her to marry him. Nor had anyone else. For ten years she had been considered the " nicest girl " in Hartwell, and numberless young men had admired her both afar and in tolerable proximity, but no man had ever told her that he loved her. No man, that is, except Mortimer G. Leffingwell, who had used that expression on the previous Sunday evening, and had asked her to accompany him to Senegambia.

She had requested two days for consideration, and this was the second day. It had been a strange experience; not at all like what she had at times imagined it would be, if it ever came to her. He had not gone down on one knee, nor was there any lovelight in his eyes; he had sat quite tranquilly with his knees crossed, and one of his feet dangling deliberately; his eyes were closed, as he formulated his proposition. Miss Millicent was conscious of a vague disappointment here, and yet she was not sure but Mr. Leffingwell would have looked ridiculous if he had chosen any other way. As it was, he had not been ridiculous at all, though perhaps a little prosaic. She suspected, however, that he was rather a matter-of-fact person, though she knew he was very bright, and that the professors considered him an ornament to the seminary. He would undoubtedly make a good husband—for someone—and she herself—well, she was no longer a school-girl, and ought not to expect a proposal in the terms of a school-girl's fancy. It was enough that he had proposed at all, was it not? All these years she had been waiting for just that, had she not? Really, that is; of course not so to be acknowledged, even to herself, up till now. But at last the door had been opened, and why should she stand hesitant before it? Her father would praise the Lord for his mercy, she was sure; her mother—in spite of the fact that Mrs. Millicent had always insisted that her chief trial in this life was to have a man around—would have rejoiced with the Deacon, had she been alive. Perhaps she knew all about it, as it was. Achsah Millicent had never felt so near her mother as she did in those two days; full of soft affection for her, and an intense longing to have her back again. Yet, after all, she reflected, the main question was not concerning parental approval, but whether she loved Mr. Leffingwell. Did she love him? She was not at all sure that she did, and yet— When she reached this point in the circle of inner argumentation, during the course of those two days, she invariably wanted to cry. For she had never loved anybody—that is, any man—that is, not since she was the merest girl— and perhaps she was now incapable of the emotion that other people seemed to feel. The happiness of it might be meant for other people; she had always had a quiet, virginal happiness of her own. And still, she was not sure. Perhaps love had to grow, like other beautiful things, and very likely respect was the proper soil for it. She certainly respected Mortimer G. Leffingwell very much indeed. Like herself, he had been early consecrated to the foreign field, and he was now expecting to give up a great deal that was tempting to him in order to go to Senegambia. Those dark faces called to him day and night, he had said; and he had added, with closed eyes, that he was sure she, too, would obey the call. And there were but two days for her answer. Oh, the time was so short! And it had already expired!

There was a sharp, uncompromising ring at Deacon Millicent's front door. Miss Achsah rose unsteadily; one hand was pressed to her side, the other fell to the table and rested on the map of Senegambia. She glanced downward at it involuntarily, and a sense of her duty flashed upon her. The providential way was made straight ; she would accept Mr. Leffingwell's offer. Slowly she moved into the front hall ; she did not wish to open the door too soon ; it seemed scarcely modest. Modest ? She caught her breath again. It was immodest to admit a man to the gentle, prim seclusion of her heart, when she more than half-suspected that she did not love him. Her answer should be " No ! " And yet she hesitated. The bell rang again, almost angrily. " Yes " or " No ? " In an agony of uncertainty, the girl took the gambler's choice : she would let Leffingwell's face settle the question, when she opened the door. If there was a certain something in it, she would marry him ; she did not know what it would be, but she felt that she could tell if it was there. She closed her eyes, an instant, then she threw the door wide open and stepped back.

Dan Jackson stood there with his red necktie and his laboriously written card. There was a determined scowl above his honest eyes ; his hair, still wet from the brush, was rigorously parted ; a flush of embarrassment was upon his freckled face. The nicest girl in Hartwell gave a little gasp ; then, with a smile that would have quite turned the head of a less inflexible visitor, she put out both hands to him.

" Why, Dan ! " she cried. " I'm so glad to see you. I—I didn't expect you. Come in ! "

She relieved him of his hat and the bevel-edged card, and offered him the best chair in the sitting-room. He sat up very straight, looking at her with admiring scrutiny. His gaze made her a trifle uncomfortable, though it pleased her, too.

" It is very good of you to come to see me, Dan," she said. " I am all alone this evening."

" Well," he remarked, with a covert meaning which she did not grasp, " I am glad of that. I didn't know that you would be." He pulled out his clean handkerchief, and without unfolding it, passed it over his forehead. The Millicent sitting-room seemed warm, and he had a great task imposed upon him.

Miss Achsah opened a window and let the cool, April night-breeze into the room. A fine rain was falling.

" Why, you came down in the rain, Dan ! " she exclaimed. " I did not notice it."

" I don't mind the rain," he said. " I haven't carried an umbrella all winter."

" Indeed ? Isn't that rather imprudent ? "

" Oh, I hate to bother with one. I had a

good umbrella, though, last fall ; a dollar-and-a-half umbrella, and one of those theologues stole it from me."

" Do you really think so ? " she said, laughingly. " That's a serious charge, Dan."

" Well, it's true," he went on, vindictively. " Those fellows will do anything ; you have to watch 'em all the time. I leave it to any academy boy."

" I'm afraid that wouldn't be quite fair. Aren't the boys just a little prejudiced ? "

" I dunno—maybe," he admitted, magnanimously. " But I ain't. I live right there with 'em, at my aunt's. I eat with 'em three times a day. I know all about 'em. I tell you, you want to look out for 'em." She was amused by his growing heat, without in the least understanding the reason of it, and she led him on a little recklessly. Any moment Mr. Leffingwell might appear at the front door.

" Why, Dan, anyone would think, to listen to you, that the theological students were criminals. Now you know better than that. You really respect them very much ; come, be honest ! "

" Respect 'em ! " he cried, incredulously. But she was looking him in the eyes and he was forced to modify his statement. " Respect

'em? Why, of course, I respect some of 'em.
There's one at the Obed house, who was sub-
stitute half-back on the Yale team. He's all
right. And one or two at our house may be all
right. But take 'em together, they make me
tired. And if a man makes you tired, Miss
Achsah, I don't see that it makes any difference
whether you respect him or not.''

She dropped her eyes a little; her fingers
were drumming on the open map, as if she were
turning over the boy's aphorism in her mind.
Dan Jackson saw that she hesitated, and he
drew a long breath, and took the plunge.

'' Now, for instance,'' he continued, dispas-
sionately, '' there's a theologue who sits opposite me at the table. He's got a head that's flat
on top, just as flat as a dirt-court. You could
play tennis on it, honestly, if it was a little big-
ger. And when he's got anything to say of
any importance, he kind of shuts his eyes and
opens his mouth and fires at you. His name is
Leffingwell. Mortimer *G.* Leffingwell. He's
going to be a missionary somewhere. And he
makes me tired. Now I want to know whether
it makes any difference whether I respect him
or not?''

She was silent an instant, and the boy, carried away by the triumphant force of his own

argument, made an incautious move. "He isn't a friend of yours, is he? I don't suppose I ought to say anything against him, if he is."

Miss Achsah detected the transparent hypocrisy. "Mr. Leffingwell is a friend of mine," she said, quietly. "I am sorry you do not like him, Dan. He is a very noble man."

Dan's heart came up in his throat. His worst fears were true, then. "Oh, that's all right," he said, weakly; "it's all right if you like him." Then, in a passion of revolt, he added: "Did you ever watch his ears wag when he eats?"

The girl laughed in spite of herself. There was no denying it; Mr. Leffingwell was occasionally ridiculous; and all the gentle proprieties of Miss Achsah's nature recognized and resented the fact, for the first time. But the boy thought she was laughing at him, and tears of helpless anger started to his eyes. He did not know what more he could say against Leffingwell; he groped among the chaos of sensations in his mind, as a diver spreads his arms uncertainly in the dim under-world. Then his fingers closed upon something.

"Well," he said, desperately, "I don't suppose it makes any difference whether I like him or not. He can get some girl to like him, and they'll go off and be missionaries. He's got a regular list of girls, and as fast as one of 'em won't have him, he just tries the next. He's tried two in the last three weeks.''

The boy's vision was so blurred that he could not see Miss Achsah's face. He got up awkwardly, too proud to let her suspect his misery. '' I suppose I must go now, Miss Millicent,'' he remarked, formally. '' I've had a very pleasant time.''

'' Dan,'' she said, rising swiftly and laying her right hand on his shoulder, with a voice that scared him by its intensity, '' are you making that up about the list ? ''

'' Honest Injun — hope to die ''— affirmed Dan, gloomily. '' The theologues were laughin' about it at supper to-night.''

Miss Achsah did not lift her right hand from the boy's shoulder, but with the left she reached around to the table behind her and noiselessly closed the map of Senegambia.

'' Dan,'' she remarked, with a tone of matter-of-fact hospitality that greatly relieved him, '' I don't believe you have to go just yet. Let's go out in the kitchen and make some molasses candy ; and if anyone calls, you can come in and say that I am engaged.''

They made candy with great glee, and in undisturbed seclusion, until the academy regulations forced Dan to take his departure, at five minutes before ten. It was quite too late for her to expect any other caller. Just as he was going out of the door, Miss Achsah, to his utter amazement, bent impulsively and kissed the boy's forehead.

.   .   .   .

Mr. Mortimer G. Leffingwell awoke the next morning with a sort of half-regret. He had intended to call upon Miss Millicent the previous evening, indeed very soon after supper—but happening to pick up a Review, he found an epoch-making article that bore—not directly perhaps, but none the less significantly—upon the second point in his statement of faith. It had interested him exceedingly, but he was able to say, when he laid it down, that it had not shaken a single clause of his own system of thought. The evening had been therefore well spent, though in his concentration upon the article, he had forgotten Miss Millicent until it was too late to think of calling upon her. He would go after dinner to-day, instead. But before dinner, as he sat by his study table, the student whose turn it was to bring the mail flung a note into his lap. Miss Millicent, while recognizing the privilege and honor extended to her, wrote that she felt compelled to decline his offer, and begged most earnestly that the subject might not be alluded to again.

Leffingwell ejaculated a line of Hebrew, and tipped back mournfully in his chair. It was a great disappointment to him. He had made up his mind that she was just the wife he needed. The fact that the two previous ones had rejected his proposals, thereby clearing the way for Miss Millicent, had looked like such an unmistakable indication of Providence ! And yet after all, he reflected, perhaps his confidence in the accuracy of the providential indicator had been well-placed, and he had simply misread the number—the minute mark, as it were, upon the matrimonial dial—at which the indicator had seemed to be temporarily arrested. He therefore took his address-book out of the drawer, but before turning to the next name on the list, he spent a moment in drawing a pencil mark, regretfully and elaborately, through the name of Number Three.

At Sesenheim

AT SESENHEIM

WE never should have gone to Sesenheim at all, if it had not been for Rhodora. It was a Saturday afternoon in June, and we— that is, Rhodora and her husband and the Scribe, who was an old friend of them both— were standing on the north side of the minster square at Strasburg, in front of an old bric-à-brac shop. There was a blaze of sunlight on the square, and it seemed as if waves of heat, reflected from the huge red sandstone minster, were fairly beating in our faces. The shop looked dark and cool. Its windows were hung with rare old weapons, curious drinking-cups in pewter and clay, odd bits of eighteenth-century china, and carved wooden crucifixes, together with peasants' rings and charms and many a queer ornament in ivory or silver. It was not a shop that a woman like Rhodora could easily pass by, and that which drew her fancy specially was a pair of silver candelabra, tiny graceful things, a trifle battered.

"How much do you think they would want for them?" she asked.

"I am sure I don't know," John answered, without enthusiasm.

"They are so lovely," she said, reflectively. "And I can just see them over our fireplace, John. Wait a minute." Then she disappeared within the shop, leaving John and the Scribe upon the scorching pavement. There was the sound of an eager dialogue, but the questions soon grew slower and more subdued, and presently Rhodora reappeared, empty-handed save for the Baedeker which now emerged from its temporary hiding-place underneath her travelling-wrap.

"Three hundred francs!" she exclaimed, with an impressive whisper. "Did you ever hear of anything equal to that?" The gentlemen were silent. "Now do you think that he could have suspected I was an American?" she demanded. "I'm sure I didn't make any mistake in the German."

Her companions laughed. "It is queer that so many shopkeepers do take you for an American," remarked John, ironically.

"Do you honestly think your bonnet looks like a German bonnet?" the Scribe ventured to ask.

Rhodora was mollified. "I hope not," she sighed, as if the idea brought some comfort with it. She stepped off from the narrow pavement, apparently to go toward the minster, and then stopped, as if surveying the city for final judgment.

"I believe I'm a little disappointed with Strasburg," she declared; "except, of course, for the cathedral. Three hundred francs for those candelabra!" She turned regretfully toward the shop windows again, and her eye fell upon the name of the owner, in faded gilt letters, above them. "Brion," she repeated. "Brion? It must be a French name. Why, Brion — who was Brion? Tell me, one of you two gentlemen." But John and the Scribe looked at each other helplessly. "Brion—why, *of course!*" exclaimed Rhodora. "Friederike Brion, Goethe's Friederike! John, Sesenheim must be near by, and I've always wanted to go there. It's so hot and dirty here; let's go to spend the Sunday at Sesenheim!"

That is how we three happened to make our pilgrimage to the quiet Alsatian village, whose sole claim to notice is that it was once the scene of a love episode more idyllic and more tenderly told than perhaps any other that ever won its gentle way into the world's literature.

It was all Rhodora's enthusiasm. We got but slight encouragement from Jean, our skeptical head-waiter at the Maison Rouge, to whom we applied for information. " Sesenheim ? " he repeated, with a head-waiter's shrug. " Il y a de bon vin rouge là bas, mais "— Clearly he knew nothing about Friederike Brion. There were no more trains that day. But Rhodora was not thus to be put down, after all her desires to visit Sesenheim, which dated back, she gravely informed us, to her school-girl days, when she had first read Goethe's Dichtung und Wahrheit, and had promptly fallen in love with Friederike. She dispatched the Scribe in search of a cheap edition of Dichtung und Wahrheit; she explained to her husband that for this once she would not object to a Sunday train ; and she had her own way in everything. To tell the truth, John, who during his summer vacation was inspecting the chemical laboratories of German universities, and the Scribe, who was keeping him lazy company, were both of them tempted by the idea of escaping for a day from the round of travel, and of going to seek an Arcadia.

We were lucky enough to find a guide to our Arcadia in the shape of a tiny book on Friederike Brion, written by Pastor Lucius of Sesenheim ; and as the early morning train carried us out of

Strasburg into the fresh greenness of the level Alsatian country, the Scribe was deputed to read the important passages from the Pastor's loving little chronicle. So with Friederike Brion in one hand and Dichtung und Wahrheit in the other, he read aloud, and gradually the story took shape : how the Strasburg student, twenty-one, brilliant, lovable, rode to Sesenheim in the autumn of 1770, and met the slender, light-haired daughter of the village pastor ; how the gentleness and the gayety of this maiden of eighteen won the student's heart, so that when he went back to Strasburg he could not rest, but must write her letters, bright, tender, and infinitely winning, and must send her verses with all the lyric passion of the " young Goethe " in them, and must ride out to Sesenheim again and again, tarrying longer at each visit, until it seemed to himself and to all as if he " belonged there ; " then how he grew restive, perhaps because his genius stung him and he knew himself to be only twenty-one, with the wide world before him ; how he leaned down from the saddle and parted with her, ill at ease himself, and not daring, probably, to tell her the truth ; how he wrote a final letter to her, only to find that her gentle answer " tore his heart," while his conscience troubled him a long time, forcing

him in Götz and Clavigo to do poetic penance;
how in journeying southward with the Duke of
Weimar, eight years later, he made a solitary
detour and visited the parsonage, to find all its
inmates unchanged toward him, and Friederike
calm and affectionate as of old, so that the next
morning, at sunrise, he rode away from Sesenheim "in peace," as he wrote the Frau von
Stein; and how after that the lovers never saw
each other again, Goethe rising steadily upon
his splendid and solitary path, and Friederike
Brion, spinster, growing old, and dying, in
1813, at her brother's house in the tiny village
of Meissenheim, having lived a life of such un-
selfish ministration and such sweetness that an
old woman who has survived into our own day
tells us that when as a child she heard about
angels, she "always thought of Aunty Brion in
a white dress," and that "the sick, and children, and old people" loved her.

Between the scraps of reading we kept looking out of the wide-opened windows of the
slowly moving train, upon the fields of hops and
the wide reaches of grain and grass, intersected
here and there by lines of heavy foliage, and
darkened by clumps of scattered woodland. To
the left were the Vosges, in a retreating blue
distance, while as we rolled northward, all

along on the right, beyond the Rhine, were the wooded summits of the Black Forest, misty yet and shadow-barred in the morning sunlight. It was Trinity Sunday, and the peasants in holiday costume thronged the station platforms, intent upon excursions to neighboring villages. Aside from the recurrent peasant laughter, the morning was perfectly still. After an hour, we passed Drusenheim. It was the place where Goethe changed horses, and the very next village was Sesenheim.

We got out. " It's much like the rest, after all," said John, as he stretched his lank body and eyed the typical modern German station, with its new, neat ugliness.

But Rhodora, holding her skirts together as she passed quickly through a stolid group of peasant women, had already started around the corner of the building. " Come," she said, " I know I shall find my way." We followed her along a foot-path through a clover field. To the left, over a fruit orchard, were the reddish-gray roof tiles of the village and the eight-sided tower of Pastor Brion's church. In a moment more we emerged upon the road, white in the glaring June sunlight, and winding its way into Sesenheim. As we passed the first houses, a girl was busily at work draping a white

cloth about a temporary roadside shrine of the
Virgin, in honor of the feast day. Oh, the
Gasthaus zum Anker was easily to be found, she
said ; and presently we reached it, standing just
where the Anker of Goethe's time stood, close
by the church.

The main room of the inn proved to be
deserted, except for the innkeeper's daughter,
and two or three peasants quietly taking their
bread and cheese and wine in a corner. The
place was scrupulously clean, with yellow-painted
tables and benches, after the Alsatian fashion.
Rhodora soon discovered on the wall a print of
the old parsonage and of the Brion family, as
the latter had existed in the idealizing mind of
some tolerable artist. The present parsonage
was modern, the Fräulein smilingly told us, but
the barn was just as it was when Goethe and
Friederike painted the old chaise together, and
had such ill luck with the varnishing ; and the
jasmine bower, where they sat in the moonlight,
was there, too. Pastor Lucius had moved away,
but his successor would be glad to show everything to us.

We had an Alsatian country dinner, with such
delicious water that even " le bon vin rouge " was
almost a superfluity, in a small room whose
window looked out on a garden, beyond which

was the old gray church. A faint smell of June roses came in from the garden. Perhaps it was only Rhodora's fancy, but it veritably seemed as if we became aware of something subtler than any rose-scent in the atmosphere of this place. There was a hint here of an immortal fragrance. During the meal we talked much of Goethe—of his capacity for loving, his impressionableness to external influences, and that reflection of his actual experiences in his poetry which makes what he has written such a revelation of the modern mind. Did his life turn once for all, here in this quiet Sesenheim, and adopt certain lines of choice? Was the Sesenheim experience a spiritual crisis for him, or was it only an incident in his development, like his love affairs with Annette and Gretchen and Lili and many another? We fell to discussing, naturally enough, his reasons for breaking faith with Friederike, and came no nearer a solution than other people have done, who have never taken dinner under the shadow of the Sesenheim church. Rhodora was inclined to be lenient with the young genius. Would it have been wise or right for him, she asked, to make this gentle country girl happy, when his future was unsettled, when the consciousness of power was strong within him, and he knew she could never keep pace

with him ?   Rhodora is a brilliant talker, especially with the odds against her, and she was
quicker than either of the men, and knew more
about Goethe.   But John burst out finally, his
brown eyes flashing, and his hand playing nervously with the last of his cherries :—

"You make one mistake, my dear : no German in Goethe's time, and hardly one in our
own, would dream that his wife could 'keep
pace with him;' and he would not want to
have her do so, even if he believed she could.
You forget where you are.   Now do you suppose," he added, almost fiercely, "that any
man of genius has the right to break the heart
of a girl like Friederike, in order to further his
own 'development'?"

"But I think, John," Rhodora answered,
slowly, "it is not a question of what is right or
wrong: it is a question of the inevitable, of
something that would lie outside the man's
will."

It seemed to the Scribe that the last word
had been said, on each side.   Perhaps the
Fräulein suspected it, too, for she came up timidly, and suggested that as there was to be a
funeral service in the church, we might make
the best of the opportunity to see the interior.
So we paid for the dinner, while Rhodora drew

on her tan-colored gloves, straightening her
bonnet stealthily before a cracked glass in the
main room of the inn, and we strolled over to
the church, entering in the wake of half a dozen
slowly pacing women.   The edifice, consisting
of a single narrow nave and rounding choir,
was built in the fifteenth century, and since the
time of Louis XIV. has been used by Roman
Catholics and Protestants alike, as is often the
custom in Alsace-Lorraine.   In the aisle was a
tombstone, with the inscription half effaced,
bearing the date of 1557, over which the young
Goethe's feet once stepped so lightly; and
there was the Pastor's pew, in which, by the
side of Friederike, he found her father's sermon " none too long."   In the apse was a tin-
selled altar, with crucifix and candles and the
image of the Virgin, while on the right wall of
the nave was the pulpit, decorated, as were all
the windows, with long green branches in
honor of Trinity Sunday.   The seats were filled
with peasant women, in dark, immobile rows ;
each dressed like all the others, in a black al-
paca gown, a short sack of the same material
edged with velvet ribbon, a brocaded silk neck-
cloth, and a queer little quilted black silk cap,
with wide, stiff bows of ribbon that stood out
from the head like the wings of a huge, dusky

butterfly. They were all of that age, from thirty to sixty-five, when peasants look just alike — their hair bleached yellow and their faces browned by labor in the fields ; shrewd faces, many of them, with strong features, but absolutely untouched by any lines of thought ; with animal patience and endurance in them, and in the eyes something of the expression that a dog or horse has when he looks at you and does not understand you. They were all hushed and reverent now, in the presence of the offices of the church.

The Lutheran Pastor ascended into the pulpit, and read the formal death notice of the person whose funeral sermon he was to preach. It was an old woman, born in the very year that Friederike Brion died. There had once been an irregularity in her life, it appeared. "My beloved ones, this woman was sinful," the round-faced blonde young Pastor began, "but we are all sinful." He paused, and there was a profound stillness. An old peasant woman on the seat in front of us turned to a companion, and whispered, the tears starting from her bleared eyes, " Das ist wahr." He went on again, preaching from the text, "Dust thou art," amid a silence almost painful. A few children sat in front of the pulpit. On the very back seat were three men, not old, but with strangely wrinkled faces, and all of them were sobbing. Through the open window near the pulpit the June breeze blew in, making the linden branches rustle gently, and throw flickering shadows on the whitewashed wall. The Scribe found himself looking at Rhodora. She sat leaning forward slightly, intent upon the unfamiliar language; her gloved hands clasped and resting in her lap, her jaunty brown jacket loosened; a touch of color in her face, her gray eyes wide and never moving from the Pastor, -her thin lips parted. Beyond this delicate, sensitive, highly organized American woman, curiously out of place here, were the rows of Alsatian peasants, whose lives were narrowed down to Sesenheim and the fields around it. "Dust thou art," the preacher kept reiterating; ay, but of what different clay, and how differently breathed upon ! Yet here, in this out-of-the-way corner of the world, in the presence of these reverent souls and these solemn words, life seemed all of a sudden very simple and to be tested by simple standards, whether the life be Goethe's or a peasant woman's.

We came out into the full glow of the afternoon. Along a stone wall that inclosed the churchyard were ranged a dozen boys, waiting for the sermon to come to an end. "Just as if it were a New England country meeting-house!" laughed John. The short grass of the churchyard was covered with small white daisies; some geese toddled away from us as we wandered around to look for the gravestones of the elder Brions, which we found leaning up against the outer wall of the church, with name and date almost illegible: and all this was more like a country churchyard in the Old England than in the New. The sexton came out soon, bringing the Protestant Bible, and a procession of white-robed girls, ready to be confirmed that afternoon in the Romanist faith, was already waiting at the door. They were homely brown little things; we looked in vain for a graceful Friederike. But Rhodora took a sudden fancy to one of them, a stooping, shy girl with great unworldly eyes, and went up and spoke to her. What she said we did not know; perhaps the Alsatian did not, but the dark sad eyes smiled for a moment, and she actually turned and nodded at Rhodora, as the awkward procession filed into the porch. Women are curious creatures.

We walked over to the parsonage and gazed at the historic barn, while John reached his long arm over the fence and plucked a blossom from the famous jasmine bush. Just as

Rhodora was protesting that she did not care to enter the new-fangled house, even to see one of Friederike's letters, the rosy-cheeked pastor appeared at the door, and asked if he could be of any service. We looked at Rhodora. She accepted the offer with prompt wilfulness, and with a superlative expression of gratitude in her queer German that must have amused the dominic. We all began to feel a little like tourists now, and rather ashamed of ourselves, though the pastor made a charming host, and explained why the old parsonage was torn down, and when the jasmine bush was transplanted, and how he had had to study Dichtung und Wahrheit in order to answer visitors' questions ; and finally he took us to his library, where some of Friederike's letters are preserved. But a yellowed old letter counts for so little after it is framed and hung ! Something, delicate and intangible, escapes. After we had put our names in the visitors' book—we were almost the only ones from America—we came away, with a consciousness that antiquarianism and curiosity, that prose, in short, had breathed its spirit for a moment upon our hitherto unspoiled Sesenheim idyl.

Fortunately, the best was yet to come. We walked down the winding white road again,

past the straggling cottages—white, too, except
where the great weather-beaten beams of the
framework were left exposed, crossing the plastered walls at all odd angles—and on out of
the village a hundred yards or so, in search of
the spot whither most German pilgrims to Sesenheim first direct their steps, the hillock where
Friederike passed many an hour in that favorite
arbor of which Goethe himself has had so much
to say. We found the place easily enough.
Some Goethe lovers have bought the hillock,
which proved to be an ancient burial-mound,
and have erected a new arbor, bearing the inscription "Friederiken Ruh, 1770–1880." It
commands a characteristic Alsatian view: in
front, to the west, the village peeping through
its abundant trees; to right and left, the wide-
sweeping fertile plains, fed by slow watercourses
and interspersed with forest land; while on the
east stretches the long line of trees that mark
the course of the Rhine, beyond which lie the
northern heights of the Black Forest, as they
group themselves brokenly about Baden-Baden.
The arbor itself was too slender to shield us
much from the June sun, so we took refuge under
a great ash in the adjacent meadow; and lying
upon the hay, mown the day before, we watched
for hours the white clouds drift across the heaven

and pile themselves into a huge, glistening mass above the Black Forest. Our talk wandered, too, apparently as inconsequently as the clouds, but it always drifted back to Goethe. Toward sundown we strolled up to the arbor again, and waited for the train which was to carry us back to Strasburg. It was a pompous sunset, with slow-fading splendors that suffused the light flecks of cloud far in the south and north, and tinged with a rim of fire the great cloud rampart above Baden. We strained our eyes toward Stras-burg, fancying that we could see the minster spire, a speck against that saffron sky, but the light faded out before we were quite sure. The wide landscape darkened gradually; we heard the nightingales in the deep woods along the Rhine. Just before the whistle of our train sounded from Niederbronn, Rhodora rose and left us for a moment. We could see her bend-ing in the dusk above one of the bushes near the arbor; then she came back with some white primroses in her hand. She gave us each one, and stuck a third through the buttonhole of her jacket. There was just one left. John took it suddenly, and, reaching up, fastened it in the lattice of Friederike's arbor. "Why, of course, John!" said Rhodora, softly. "The poor girl!" Then she took John's arm, and we came away.

WOMAN'S ASSOCIA

www.ingramcontent.com/pod-product-compliance
Lightning Source LLC
Chambersburg PA
CBHW060600030726
47498CB00005B/1471

* 9 7 8 3 7 4 4 6 6 1 1 3 3 *